SUPERMAN
R E T U R N S™

STRANGE VISITOR

by Louise Simonson

An original story inspired by the film *Superman Returns*

Screenplay by
Michael Dougherty & Dan Harris

Story by
Bryan Singer & Michael Dougherty & Dan Harris

Superman created by Jerry Siegel and Joe Shuster

PUFFIN

PUFFIN BOOKS

Published by the Penguin Group
Penguin Books Ltd, 80 Strand, London WC2R ORL, England
Penguin Group (USA) Inc., 375 Hudson Street, New York, New York 10014, USA
Penguin Group (Canada), 90 Eglinton Avenue East, Suite 700, Toronto, Ontario, Canada M4P 2Y3
(a division of Pearson Penguin Canada Inc.)
Penguin Ireland, 25 St Stephen's Green, Dublin 2, Ireland (a division of Penguin Books Ltd)
Penguin Group (Australia), 250 Camberwell Road, Camberwell, Victoria 3124, Australia
(a division of Pearson Australia Group Pty Ltd)
Penguin Books India Pvt Ltd, 11 Community Centre, Panchsheel Park, New Delhi – 110 017, India
Penguin Group (NZ), cnr Airborne and Rosedale Roads, Albany, Auckland 1310, New Zealand
(a division of Pearson New Zealand Ltd)
Penguin Books (South Africa) (Pty) Ltd, 24 Sturdee Avenue, Rosebank, Johannesburg 2196, South Africa

Penguin Books Ltd, Registered Offices: 80 Strand, London WC2R ORL, England

penguin.com

First published in the USA by Little, Brown and Company 2006
First published in Great Britain by Puffin Books 2006
2

Made and printed in England by Clays Ltd, St Ives plc

British Library Cataloguing in Publication Data
A CIP catalogue record for this book is available from the British Library

ISBN-13: 978-0-141-32170-7
ISBN-10: 0-141-32170-9

Prologue

The crime scene was blocked off. Yellow Metropolis Police Department tape stretched across the door of the drug-manufacturing lab at Galaxy Pharmaceuticals to prevent unauthorized entry.

Broken glass from the shattered floor-to-ceiling windows littered the linoleum. Overturned equipment cluttered cabinet tops and spilled onto the floor. Bullet holes pocked the walls.

A man and a woman wearing white jumpsuits scoured the surfaces with magnifying glasses. Large black labels on their backs read M.P.D.: Metropolis Police Department. But labels can lie.

"Sure, Superman fought a pitched battle here with that drug gang. And kicked their butts. But what makes

Dr. Vale so sure we'll find Superman's DNA?" the man grumbled.

"Think, Chuck," the woman hissed. "This is a lab — as sterile an environment as any we'll find. That's why they sent us here and not to any of the hundreds of other places where Superman has stopped crimes in the past few months."

"Yeah," Chuck mumbled. "When people fight, they bleed. We've found plenty of evidence of that! But Superman doesn't bleed. Bullets bounce off him."

"Which is why they want his DNA," the woman retorted. "Superman has powers — extraordinary powers — and Vale wants to find the source of them."

"Source?" Chuck echoed. "The guy's an alien from the planet Krypton — wherever that is!"

The woman sighed. "The source of his abilities is inborn, coded into his DNA. Wherever living beings are, human or alien, they shed bits of themselves — hairs, flakes of skin. Vale wants us to find a piece of Superman that he can analyze."

She picked up a hair with a pair of tweezers and studied it through a jeweler's loupe.

She placed it in a sterile envelope and moved on to study the next square foot of lab space.

After a moment, Chuck grumbled, "Only one thousand square feet to go."

Project Cadmus was a vast underground complex that ran deep beneath a mountain northwest of Metropolis. It housed a cutting-edge private scientific research organization, partially funded by government contracts. Its specialties ranged from robotics to genetics, from astrophysics to weaponry.

No single employee, including Chief of Robotics Research, Dr. Emmet Vale, was aware of the scope of its operations. The Project Cadmus directors had planned it that way. Above all else, they valued secrecy.

Ceiling-mounted cameras swiveled as Dr. Vale stepped from the elevator onto Cadmus Level Three.

"Superman's presence on Earth poses a clear and present danger," Vale lectured as he led three members of the secret Senate Select Committee for Extraterrestrial Threat Analysis down the long hall toward his robotics lab. "He can't be coerced, controlled, or brought under the influence of the United States government."

"You said it!" Bulldog-faced Senator Buckram scowled. "Superman stops a robbery or prevents a train crash, then he disappears. We don't know where he goes or what he does next, since he moves too quickly for radar to track him. And he's more powerful than anything the military can throw at him."

"So far," Vale said smoothly, and he smiled his thin-lipped smile. "That's why you've commissioned Project Cadmus to create anti-Superman devices —"

"To be deployed in case the blasted alien ever loses it!" thin, wiry Senator Liddel interrupted nervously.

"Superman has worked hard to become Earth's hero and win the trust of the world." Vale's eyeglasses caught the light, giving him a maniacal look. "When he makes his move to take over this planet — and believe me, gentlemen, he will, for why else would an alien of his enormous power *be* here? — the United States government must be ready to stop him."

Dr. Vale palmed a hand plate beside a metal door.

4

Shwisp! The door slid open and Vale led the senators into a large workroom cluttered with computers and high-tech tools.

"This way," Vale said. The senators followed him to the center of the room, where a figure shrouded in a white sheet lay on a metal gurney.

"When the time comes, we'll have a two-pronged approach," Vale explained. "Our first step will be to destroy Superman. This — Metallo — will be our weapon."

Vale whipped back the sheet, revealing a gleaming metal robot. Metallo looked like a massive human skeleton with hydraulically driven muscles sculpted in silver. The top of its skull-like head was open and empty, as was the robot's chest cavity.

"The robot is near completion," Vail explained. "Our next step will be to select the human brain donor and perfect the power source. Then Metallo will be operational."

"You say this . . . *thing* will be able to take out Superman?" Senator Buckram sneered.

"The robot is constructed of a nanometal that makes it almost indestructible and allows it to communicate with local computer systems. It will be stronger, faster, and smarter than Superman and nearly as invulnerable," Dr. Vale assured him. "Given the right power source, when the time comes, Metallo will easily destroy the so-called Man of Steel."

If it were up to Vale, they wouldn't wait until that alien monster provoked an attack. In his view, a pre-emptive strike was called for, before Superman used his power to threaten everything they held dear.

"As you know, the second part of our plan is to re-place Superman with a doppelgänger," Vale continued.

He led the senators back into the hall and onto an elevator. He pushed a button that would take them several levels deeper into Project Cadmus.

"This operation has been trickier," Vale explained. "So far, much of Superman's DNA has resisted our structural analysis, so we've been forced to make substi-tutions based on our best guesses."

He led the senators into a second lab. This one con-tained a large glass vat in which a massive, chalk-white, man-shaped body floated in clear liquid. Wires led to electrodes attached to the being's skull and body and snaked up to the top of the tank.

"What's this?" Senator Buckram barked.

"This is Bizarro Mark 3," Vale explained. "The creature is constructed of nanoparticles: tiny molecule-sized machines that mimic what we know of Superman's DNA."

"This . . . *monster* is supposed to replace Superman in the hearts and minds of America's citizens?" Senator Liddel was incredulous.

"The creature isn't Superman, obviously," Vale replied coldly. "But it is something very like Superman. Once it is awakened, it will mimic his powers of flight and heat vision, of superhearing and invulnerability. It will perform Superman's usual rescue functions. And, most important of all, it will be fully under Pentagon control. In time, the public will accept Bizarro as its hero, as they now accept Superman."

Gazing at Bizarro, Senator Liddel looked more revolted than convinced.

"And when will these . . . creatures — Metallo and

Bizarro — be ready for activation?" the third senator, a gray-haired woman with a long witch's nose, asked briskly.

She had pinpointed Vale's one area of concern. He had not yet found the perfect brain donor for Metallo . . . or the perfect power source. And he was already over budget. He needed to produce results quickly or they would withdraw his financing.

So he smiled and said, "Soon, senators. You will be invited to watch Metallo's brain transplant within the next few months."

1

Superman flew above Metropolis, his city. His home. Home of the people he protected and served.

Below him, horns blared. Traffic crawled forward. Cabs snaked in and out of lanes, trying to get one space ahead. Pedestrians thronged sidewalks and hurried through crosswalks. Some looked up and waved and Superman grinned and waved down at them.

He climbed higher, enjoying the feeling of autumn sunlight on his skin.

For Superman, basking in sunlight was more than a pleasant pastime. In some ways, it made him who he was. His body was like a living solar battery and Earth's yellow sun energized him and gave him powers far beyond those of ordinary humans.

Real humans, he thought suddenly. And his stomach lurched.

The realization generally came upon him when he least expected it, brought him down when he was flying high.

The memory of what he was: an alien on Earth. The last of his kind. A part-time imposter passing as human reporter Clark Kent. A man living a lie.

Shortly after he was born, his Kryptonian parents, knowing the world of his birth was doomed, had put him in a crystal rocket ship and sent him to the planet Earth. Behind him, the red sun of Krypton had gone nova, and the planet of his birth had been destroyed. Everyone on Krypton had died.

His Kryptonian parents had been right to count on the basic kindness of Earth's denizens. His rocket ship had crashed in a cornfield on Martha and Jonathan Kent's farm, and the childless couple had taken him in and raised him as their own son.

Until he was twelve, he had thought he *was* their son. It had never occurred to him that he was anything other than human.

Until the day he flew.

His Kryptonian parents had known Earth's yellow sun would make him a superman. His father, Jor-El, had believed his superhuman powers would help him survive.

But his mother, Lara, had worried, wisely, that they would also make him feel different and alone. . . .

∞   ∞   ∞

A fire alarm ringing somewhere in the city jolted Superman back to the present. He listened carefully, focusing his superhearing, trying to locate the source of the sound.

Somewhere in the West 30s, he decided.

Added to the alarm, he could now hear sirens as fire engines inched through gridlocked streets.

He searched the area with X-ray vision until he spotted the fire in a storage area on the third floor of Grimbly's Department Store.

As he dove toward the blaze, he saw shoppers rushing out of Grimbly's like ants from a disturbed anthill. A third-floor window shattered, raining down glass on the pedestrians and adding to the panic and confusion.

Smoke poured from the opening.

Superman glided through the window frame into an inferno. Flames shot up the wall and licked hungrily across the floor and ceiling. Half the boxes in the storeroom were ablaze.

Superman took a deep breath and blew as hard and fast as he was able.

Like candles in the wind, the flames flickered . . . and died.

"Good job," a woman's voice said from a side door. "You just saved the new fall line from destruction . . . not to mention about a thousand jobs that would have been lost if the store had to shut down."

Superman glanced toward the doorway. And smiled.

Lois Lane, star reporter for the *Daily Planet,* stood clutching a Grimbly's bag and grinning back at him. She was dressed in a trim russet suit and her dark hair fell in waves to her shoulders. As usual, the sight of her took his breath away.

"I was here buying a sweater," she said. "Looks like I can't avoid breaking stories, even on my lunch hour."

Superman nodded. "You know, Lois, you should have left the building when the alarm sounded."

Lois frowned. "I started to. But when I reached this floor, I smelled the smoke. And I began to wonder about the source of the fire and why no sprinklers had gone off. So I —"

"Had to find out," Superman finished. "And have you?"

"Have I what?" Lois asked, stepping closer and gazing into his eyes.

"Have you found out about the sprinklers?"

"Not yet," Lois answered. "But I will."

∞   ∞   ∞

Lois Lane burst through the swinging doors into the Daily Planet bull pen, her curls flying. She rushed past editors and copyboys, photographers and reporters. The smell of FatBoy burgers, take-out Chinese, and pizza wafted through the room as journalists wolfed down fast food lunches at their desks while banging out stories for the evening edition.

Ignoring the hum of voices and the drone of wall-mounted TV monitors showing breaking news from around the world, she made a beeline for editor in chief Perry White's office.

As she stuck her head in the open doorway, she rattled off, "Got you a page one exclusive, Chief! Superman just put out a fire at Grimbly's Department Store. Used superbreath. He saved the building single-handed. The sprinklers had been disabled and arson is suspected —"

The gray-haired editor in chief looked up from the stack of photos he'd been studying. Jimmy Olsen, the copyboy, was standing beside Perry's chair, pointing to one of the photos and looking hopeful.

Jimmy pushed back the reddish-blond hair that had flopped in his face and grinned. "Hi, Miss Lane!"

"Hey, Jimmy!"

Jimmy Olsen had talked his way into a copyboy's job, fresh out of high school, but Lois knew he really wanted to be a photographer. She suspected that Perry was now holding a stack of Jimmy's most recent photos, and that Jimmy was, once again, trying to sell Perry on one of them.

Perry White glanced down at the photos, then up at Lois. "You get any pictures?" he asked.

Lois rolled her eyes. "I'm a reporter, Chief, not a photographer."

Perry pushed back his chair and glared at Lois. "And I publish newspapers, not novels. Jimmy, get over to Grimbly's and take some shots of the damage there."

"Gosh, golly, thanks, Chief," Jimmy stammered. "I'll just grab my camera and —" He dashed from the room.

"And don't call me 'chief!'" Perry shouted after him.

∞ ∞ ∞

An hour later, Clark Kent strolled down the center aisle of the bullpen and settled into his desk beside Lois's.

He smiled smugly at the sight of Lois, bent over her keyboard, typing furiously. "What's up?" he asked.

"Superman," she muttered without looking over at him. "Fire. Superbreath."

Clark grinned. One of the most enjoyable things about being Superman was having Lois report on his exploits. But he couldn't let her get all the stories or he'd lose his spot as her most successful rival.

15

"Guess you missed the aborted air crash at Metropolis Airport," Clark said as he began to type. "Superman got there just in time!"

"What?!" Lois squinted at him suspiciously. "How do you know? What were you doing there?"

"I listened to the police bands," Clark said, not looking up from the keyboard. "And I went there like a good reporter should."

Lois squinted her eyes. "Did you get an exclusive interview?"

"Sure!" Clark typed a while longer, keeping her in suspense. Then he admitted, "With eyewitnesses. Not with Superman himself. By the time I got there, he was long gone."

"Good," Lois muttered and went back to her own story.

"Of course, I have *pictures,*" Clark said, stifling a grin. "A tourist with a digital camera and a telephoto lens must have taken two dozen shots. I'm forwarding them to Perry so he can select a few and pay the guy. I'd say they're page-one material."

2

"Good work, Kent! Lois!" Perry White said as the sky outside his window darkened toward dusk. Their Superman stories sat on his desk, side by side.

Jimmy Olsen rushed into Perry's office. "Got your pictures, Chief!" He plopped the photos of the charred storeroom down on Perry's desk. He looked expectantly from Perry White to Lois.

Then he saw the tourist's Superman photos on Perry's desk and his face fell.

"Kent, your story and picture go on page one above the fold," Perry said. "Lois, your article on the bottom. Olsen, we'll run one of your shots with the conclusion of Lois's story on page five."

Jimmy grinned in relief. "Thanks, Chief!" It was his first sale and he was ecstatic.

Lois frowned. "Perry, do you ever wonder if the *Daily Planet* has become too dependent on Superman to sell papers?"

Perry humphed. "I'll worry about sales. You just keep the Superman exclusives coming."

"A lot of good that did me this time," she muttered.

Clark glanced at Lois in surprise. "Don't tell me you're getting bored with Superman?"

"Not likely! He's . . ." Lois sighed dreamily. Then she frowned. "I just wonder if it's smart to put all our eggs in one basket. Superman stories and pictures, above and below the fold. Surely there are other things happening in the world."

"If there are, they aren't your problem! Superman's what our readers care about!" Perry frowned. "Where is this coming from anyway? If it's because Kent beat you out —"

Lois thrust out her chin and folded her arms. "It's a reasonable concern."

Clark knew that look. Lois had just accepted the challenge, even if Perry didn't realize he'd made one.

Jimmy frowned. As great as he thought Superman

was, he figured Miss Lane had a point. "The Web's buzzing with rumors that the *Starfarer* satellite has intercepted a distress signal from deep space. Why aren't we investigating that?"

Perry looked toward the heavens for patience. "Stick to photographs, Olsen. We'll let the *National Whisper* cover that one."

"You know, Jimmy, that interplanetary-distress-signal idea wasn't bad," Lois muttered as they left Perry White's office several minutes later.

She snatched her purse from her desk and raced toward the exit. "I'll check it out. Try to get some scientist's take on it —"

"Miss Lane! Wait!" Jimmy called. He grabbed his camera and rushed after her. "Let me come with you. I could take photos —"

"No way!" Lois said. Seeing his disappointed look, she rephrased her refusal. "Not right now, Jimmy. If something comes of it, you'll get your shot. I promise."

"Hey, Olsen," old Jack Green called from his desk in

the far corner of the room. "This obit photo needs to get to layout ASAP."

"Yeah. Okay," Jimmy mumbled. He slouched toward the obituary writer's desk as Lois sprinted out the swinging doors.

Clark glanced after her. Lois had a true investigative reporter's feel for a story. If she thought the distress signal was worth looking into, there was a good chance she was right.

Instinctively, he pulled his glasses down his nose and stared upward with X-ray vision through the many floors of the Daily Planet building. He engaged his telescopic vision and stared off into space.

It was a reflex action. He knew the *Starfarer* unmanned space exploration satellite was far beyond Earth's solar system and that, powerful though his supersenses were, they couldn't penetrate into the depths of space.

He spotted the approaching meteors as the news service on the wall-mounted TV crackled out a warning: ". . . NASA scientists have raised an emergency alert, announcing an unexpected bombardment of large meteors across the northeastern coast of the United States. . . ."

Clark knew the streaks of light most people called "shooting stars" were actually tiny meteors, bits of cosmic debris entering the atmosphere at extremely high speeds. Most were smaller than a grain of sand and burned away long before they hit the ground.

But the rocks Clark was staring at were more like boulders, varying in size from tiny pebbles to Mack trucks.

Ignoring the reporters crowding around him and the TV, Clark leaped to his feet and strode purposefully out through the bullpen's swinging doors, sprinted past the elevators, and slipped into the stairwell at the end of the hall.

He raced up fifty flights of stairs at superspeed, frantically ripping off suit, shirt, and tie to expose the skintight blue Superman suit he always wore beneath his clothing. Finally, he burst through the access door onto the roof of the Daily Planet building.

For a moment, he stood beneath the revolving globe

that was the newspaper's famous symbol. His bright red cape waved in the breeze as he stared toward space.

Then he leaped into the sky and soared straight upward. As he flew, he thought about what he would have to do.

Engage the meteors at the highest point, he told himself. *Destroy the largest meteors first, the ones that are likely to do the most damage. Above all, protect Metropolis.*

He soared through the stratosphere and into the mesosphere, where millions of tiny particles of space debris burned up every day. Fifty miles above the earth he reached the ionosphere, and it was here that he encountered the leading edge of the meteor shower — a rain of pebbles and small rocks which he swept over with a wide arc of heat vision that melted them to slag.

Tumbling behind these, fast and furious, came larger rocks that varied from the size of basketballs to SUVs and even train cars.

Flying at superspeed, he zigged and zagged in the air above Metropolis, melting smaller meteors with heat vision, smashing larger ones into dust with his fists. He ignored the meteors that would fall into the ocean and concentrated on destroying the ones that threatened the city.

Lois Lane stopped her red sports car by the guardhouse at the entrance to Project Cadmus, the secretive research complex in Kirby County, thirty miles northwest of Metropolis. She presented her identification and, while she waited for the armed guard to check her press ID and authorization, she studied the setup carefully.

The forested mountaintop site intrigued her. If not for the guards and the barbed-wire fence surrounding the property, a casual observer would never suspect it held anything of importance.

The guard handed back her ID and pointed her toward a flat-roofed, single-story brick building on the edge of the forest. Her interview with a Project Cadmus radio astronomer would take place inside.

As Lois slowly pulled away from the guardhouse, she knew she was driving on top of the real Cadmus. The main complex was underground, and she suspected its roots ran wide and deep, maybe even as far as Metropolis. She had heard rumors of strange experiments and even stranger results taking place within its labs.

During her time at the *Daily Planet*, she had looked for a reason to enter the complex but had never found one — until now. She realized she would never be allowed beyond this upper, public level. She could hardly believe she'd snared an interview, even on so harmless a subject as a possible signal from outer space.

As she parked in the visitor slot, something that sounded like hail rattled on the roof of her car.

"Weird," she muttered.

Peering up through the windshield, she saw a bright flash of light cross the evening sky, followed by another. Meteors. Falling stars.

As she climbed from her car, she smiled and made a wish.

3

Fifty miles above Metropolis, a meteor as large as a house tumbled toward Superman. He plowed into it at super-speed, using his invulnerable body as a battering ram. The giant rock shattered into a hundred smaller chunks which he followed downward, smashing, pounding, melting as he flew thirty miles above the earth . . . twenty . . . ten.

A cluster of car-sized meteors appeared simultaneously.

He hurled himself at them, smashing through them, striking at superspeed, again and again, until they, too, were pulverized.

But even as he destroyed these, others zipped past him, and he realized there was no way he could stop them all. He was going to have to narrow his focus:

destroy the largest meteors and deal with damage from the smaller ones later.

∞   ∞   ∞

Lois walked through sliding doors into an austere reception area that gave no hint of the technical marvels rumored to exist underneath.

An efficient-looking gray-haired woman whose nameplate said Carrie Adams was seated behind a black metal desk.

Lois smiled. "Lois Lane, Miss Adams. I'm here for an interview."

"Dr. Welles will be right with —"

WHAMB! The receptionist's words disappeared in an explosion as half the ceiling crashed inward.

Lois threw herself onto the floor as one end of a concrete roof slab caught on the edge of the receptionist's desk above her and the other end slammed onto the floor beside her.

Lois lay sheltered by a makeshift lean-to as the ground beneath her trembled. She was deafened by rattles, pops, and roars. From nearby, she caught the smell of hot, burning metal.

What is it? A terrorist attack? An earthquake? Lois wondered. She raised her head, but all she could see was grit-covered debris. Dust burned her eyes and nose and clogged her mouth.

The rattle of something — stones? — against the slab overhead reminded her of the earlier noise on her car roof. And the shooting stars.

Surely this can't be some huge meteor shower, she thought. *Can it?*

A second barrage shook the ground. From underground, Lois heard the faint blare of an alarm.

With a screech of metal, the near legs of the desk gave way. The huge slab above Lois's head began to slide sideways.

Lois dove from beneath it seconds before it smashed onto the floor.

The receptionist was lying unconscious beside her desk, half buried in roof debris. Her face was covered in grit and her head was bleeding.

27

Lois crawled toward her over trembling ground.

A door burst open and a man in a white lab coat stepped out. Beyond him, a stairway led down to a lower level. With the door open, the alarm from below was deafening.

"Carrie!" the man called.

"She's here!" Lois shouted. "She's hurt! Help me get this concrete off her!"

The man stumbled across the wreckage, and together they moved the debris and pulled the woman free.

Lois grabbed one of her arms, the man in the lab coat grabbed the other, and they carried her into the depths of Project Cadmus.

Several floors below, in a high-tech operating theater, Dr. Emmet Vale and his team of surgical assistants had removed the living brain from a volunteer. They were now preparing to insert it into the silver skull of the robot Metallo.

Months before, the criminal John Corben's spinal cord had been severed and much of his body crushed when he crashed his car while escaping from police. Without the machines that kept his body functioning, Corben would already be dead. There was no chance that he would ever recover and so he had jumped at the chance to reacquire mobility, even in a strange and experimental form.

Corben's body now lay on one operating table, covered with a sheet, as Vale and his team of assistants surrounded the Metallo body. The robot body was, at present, drawing power from Project Cadmus. Corben's living brain was in Vale's hands.

Dr. Vale scowled as he began the insertion. He wasn't satisfied with Corben's mental and emotional profile. Nor had he solved the problem of providing the permanent power source Metallo would need to be one-hundred-percent effective.

Perhaps that's just as well, Vale thought. *If Corben proves to be an inadequate choice, I can unplug him and find another brain donor. In the meantime, this will keep the senators off my back.*

He glanced up at the glass-enclosed observation area where the three senators were seated.

As Vale inserted the first electrodes that would act as an artificial spinal cord to read and transfer the brain's impulses to the robot's body, the floor lurched violently.

The walls trembled, and an alarm began to howl. The lights blinked off, then on again at half power.

A machine beside the robot began to shriek.

"We've lost energy!" Vale's main assistant cried. "Brain/blood oxygen levels are falling. We're losing electrical activity. Cerebral blood flow is negative."

The safety glass surrounding the observation area exploded. Pellets of glass rained down on Vale, his assistants, and the robot, Metallo, further damaging Corben's brain.

"What's happening?" Senator Buckram shouted. "Sounds like World War III just broke out!"

"Dr. Vale," a calm voice from an intercom interrupted. "We're experiencing a violent meteor shower. The upper labs are being evacuated. If you and the senators will go into the corridors, you'll be directed to safe areas in the lower levels."

"Bring the robot," Vale snapped as he dropped Corben's damaged, useless brain into a metal container and pulled off his surgical gloves.

Obediently, Vale's assistants threw a sheet over the robot and shoved the gurney into the hall.

As the floor shook again, the three senators scrambled from the observation area and rushed after them.

∞   ∞   ∞

The alarm shrieked and the walls rattled as Lois Lane and the lab-coated scientist carried the injured receptionist to the floor below. There they joined a stream of uniformed humanity: guards, doctors, scientists, even some suited bureaucrats. Many of them, like Lois, were covered with dust. Some were clutching vats, boxes, files — whatever they could salvage of their most important projects.

Thousands of people must work for Cadmus, Lois realized. *How did the project maintain such tight secrecy?*

Leaving Lois and Carrie leaning against a wall, the scientist dashed into a lab and came out with a wheelchair. They draped the unconscious receptionist in it, then followed the stream of humanity down another level.

The ceiling creaked ominously. "Be careful what you wish for," Lois muttered to herself. For years, she had tried to get inside Project Cadmus. But now that she was here, she wondered if going below ground was a terrible mistake.

The ground shook. *Another impact!* Lois thought uneasily. If one roof could collapse, what would keep the others from pancaking along with it? The farther underground they went, the deeper they might get buried.

A grim-looking group of surgeons shoved a sheet-shrouded gurney into the retreating mass of people, half-blocking the corridor and separating Lois from the scientist and receptionist. A corner of the sheet flipped back, exposing a metal hand.

Three people in suits crowded behind them. One of them looked like Senator Buckram of Texas. . . . *What would he be doing here?*

She followed the sloping corridor down another level. *WHRAMPPP!*

The ground shook — harder than it did before. A crack began to form along the middle of the ceiling. Dust crumbled onto the people packing the hallway.

Then, with a ripping sound, the ceiling down the corridor gave way, plunging the hall into darkness.

4

Hovering in the mesosphere, Superman zipped back and forth, desperately pulverizing one huge meteor after another. Twenty-two . . . twenty-three . . .

He looked around for more . . . and saw nothing.

He searched the heavens above Metropolis with telescopic vision. For as far as he could see, local space was clear of anything larger than a grain of sand.

He soared upward, into the ionosphere, above the shadow of the earth. He still saw nothing.

For a moment he hovered there, absorbing the rays of the setting sun and recharging his depleted powers. Then he arched backward and dove toward Metropolis.

As he fell, he scanned the city with telescopic vision, searching for signs of damage. A few small meteorites had gotten past him and smashed through windows or hammered the roofs of parked cars but, for the most part, Metropolis had been spared.

The power was on. The rotating globe on top of the Daily Planet building was spinning slowly. All was right with his city.

He breathed a sigh of relief.

As he dropped lower still, he heard the faint sound of an alarm. It was muffled, even to his superhearing, as if it was coming from beneath the ground. Puzzled, Superman hovered, searching for its source.

He found it: Project Cadmus, situated in the low mountains northwest of the city. As he flew closer, he saw that the surrounding barbed-wire fence had been mangled in places and the guardhouse at the entrance had been slightly damaged.

A single-story building had been half destroyed by a meteorite several feet wide. In the parking lot was a dented red sports car.

Lois drives a car like that, he thought. *She was researching the distress-signal story. Could she have come to Cadmus?*

He tightened his focus on the car's bumper and recognized Lois's license-plate number.

Frantically, he searched the smashed building with X-ray vision. He spotted Lois's purse, crushed flat beneath a fallen concrete slab.

The alarm! he thought suddenly. *It's coming from below ground. Maybe* —

He looked down . . . and his X-ray vision stopped three feet below the surface. He realized Cadmus had lined its entire complex with lead — the one substance his X-ray vision couldn't penetrate.

What are they hiding? he wondered.

Not that it mattered, he decided. He wrenched open the door in the still-standing wall. Lois was in there. He hoped. And he was going to find her.

He dropped down into the darkness.

He searched with thermal vision as he flew down the deserted main corridor, seeing heat signatures instead of shape and color. The corridor was littered with dust, fallen chunks of ceiling, and scattered papers. Lois was nowhere in sight.

He followed a ramp down to a second level, passing offices and labs, searching for the injured. Searching for Lois.

In a small operating theater covered with shards of glass, he spotted the corpse of a man lying on an operating table. Most of the bones in the corpse's body had been broken. His skull had been opened and his brain lay in a container nearby.

A dissection, Superman mused. He shrugged and flew on.

As he dropped down a ramp to the next level, small emergency lights in the floor flickered on.

The corridor was one long ramp, he realized, circling downward as it followed the contour of the mountain. Up ahead he spotted major damage — collapsed walls and ceilings blocking a hallway.

Superman spun, tunneling through the rocky debris with his body at superspeed until he broke out on the other side.

The alarm stopped suddenly.

Then Superman heard shrieks and groans rising from somewhere below. He flew downward.

His heart nearly stopped when he heard Lois scream.

∞   ∞   ∞

Lois squinted at the dim lights that lined the corridor and tried to peer through the dusty haze and past the crowd all around her. Shortly before, above the shriek of the alarm, she had heard a loud creaking noise in the darkness, followed by a crash, and screams of pain and horror.

What had happened?

Up ahead, just beyond the doctors with their gurney and its hidden occupant, the ceiling had collapsed. Heaven knew how many people had been buried beneath that rubble. Her instinct was to rush toward the wreckage and try to free anyone who might be trapped beneath it.

Then she spotted the crack in the ceiling. She watched it grow, lengthen, move toward her, then past her up the corridor.

With an audible creak, the ceiling sagged.

"More of the ceiling is going to come down!" Lois screamed. "Back! We need to go back the way we came!"

No one heard her over the clamor of voices.

She tried to turn around, but the press of bodies held her firmly in place.

We're going to die, she thought. *Crushed like the people ahead of us in the corridor. We're going to be buried alive!*

Then, in the dim light she saw something . . . someone . . . moving. Flying. Up near the ceiling, above the heads of the crowd.

"Superman!" she screamed. "The ceiling!"

❦   ❦   ❦

Superman saw the danger. He hovered, bracing the sagging roof beams with his own body.

"Go back up to the surface," he shouted to the people below him. "The meteor shower's over. I've cleared a path through the debris in the upper corridor. Hurry! The ceiling here is about to come down!"

Superman got the crowd's attention whereas Lois had not. The people turned and began to move, slowly at first, then more rapidly, up the corridor and out of danger.

Lois pressed against the wall, watching as the crowd rushed past. With Superman nearby, she was no longer afraid.

"People are trapped," she shouted. "Up ahead where the ceiling's already come down."

"I'll get to them, Miss Lane," he answered, "after everyone is out of here — including you!"

There was a loud grinding sound as concrete and timbers settled overhead. Dust, debris, and even small rock fragments fell from the cracked ceiling onto the floor.

Superman sagged. He stretched his arms wide, trying to brace up the entire ceiling until the evacuation was complete.

But his vision was blurring. He was sweating. His arms had begun to tremble with effort.

What's wrong with me? he wondered faintly.

He saw doctors in green scrubs beside a gurney, the last people to leave.

"Go on," he croaked. "Hurry!"

The younger doctors tried to shove the gurney forward but their gray-haired leader held them back. "No! It's mine! Keep him away from it!" Superman could hear the loathing in the man's voice.

"Go!" Superman said, more weakly. "Can't . . . hold it up . . . much longer."

"Dr. Vale!" A younger doctor tugged at the older man's arm. "We have to move!"

"No!" Vale insisted. He glared up at Superman. "You don't belong here, you alien monster! You extraterrestrial fiend!"

Monster, Superman thought dimly. *Why . . . ?*

The ceiling sagged even further. More debris crashed onto the floor.

The assistants glanced nervously from Vale to Superman to the ominously sagging ceiling. Abandoning their boss, the young surgeons sprinted up the corridor.

"Go!" Superman croaked. To Lois. To the stubborn gray-haired doctor. "Something's . . . wrong. Can't hold it up . . . can't . . ."

He crashed to the floor as his strength faded. "Something's wrong," he whispered.

With the last fading remnant of his X-ray vision he found the source of his problem. Glowing green crystals were embedded in the meteorite fragments that littered the floor.

"Kryptonite!" he gasped. The meteorite that had crashed through the ceiling was an amalgam of space debris containing shattered shards of his destroyed home world — crystals that had been irradiated when Krypton's red star went nova. Fleetingly, he realized how lucky he was that the other meteorites he'd encountered were kryptonite-free. Had he been felled earlier, the city would have been left unprotected.

"Kryptonite!" Vale murmured. He stared at the rocks. It was a well-known fact that kryptonite, though harmless to humans, was a deadly poison to Superman.

"Come on!" Lois urged as she pulled Superman to his feet. "You've done all you can here!" She glared at Vale. "If we stay here, we'll die! Hurry!"

When Superman swayed, she threw her arms around his chest and half-dragged him down the corridor.

Behind her, Lois heard Dr. Vale scream. Then, with a loud rumble, the ceiling crashed around them.

5

Had they been closer to the kryptonite, the falling ceiling would have crushed them both. But Lois had gotten Superman far enough away. A portion of his strength, speed, and invulnerability had returned.

Despite his residual weakness, he threw himself on top of Lois and braced his arms, as concrete slabs smashed down on them. He sheltered her beneath his body until rescuers arrived to dig them out.

As Cadmus personnel pulled off the final debris, Superman sat back, still dizzy and disoriented.

Lois smiled up at him. "You saved my life."

He staggered to his feet, then pulled her up beside him. "It's a life worth saving," he said. Suddenly he grinned down at her, his teeth gleaming white in his grimy face. "But this time, I'd say we're even."

He looked down the blocked corridor where Cadmus guards were tunneling industriously. "I've got to help," he said.

"No, sir!" A Cadmus official stepped in front of him. "We have personnel coming at this mess from the other side of the cave-in. Thank you for your assistance, but we'll handle things from here."

He peered at Lois closely. "Miss Lane?" he asked. She was hard to recognize beneath all the dust.

Lois nodded.

The guard checked something off on his clipboard. "Cadmus personnel will escort both of you to the surface."

Superman was torn. Buried though the kryptonite was, he could still feel its poisonous effects. But people were buried there, too. With enormous effort, he summoned his X-ray vision.

Surprisingly few people lay beneath the rubble of that first collapse. Some were dead. And Cadmus personnel could reach the few survivors on the fringes more quickly than he could in his present state.

"Dig there," Superman said, pointing toward the center of the corridor. "There's a doctor . . . half under a concrete block . . . still alive."

Just activating his X-ray vision had worn him out, Superman realized. He sighed and turned away.

⚮   ⚮   ⚮

"Those ungrateful jerks!" Lois muttered as she walked beside him toward the exit. "They're dismissing you with barely a thank-you! And after all you did here, after all the lives you saved!"

"It makes you wonder," Superman murmured.

"Yeah," Lois agreed. "What's down here that Cadmus doesn't want you to see?"

"Could be they're mad at me," he said suddenly. "Protecting Metropolis was my first priority. I tried to stop the largest meteors from striking outside the city, but a few got away from me."

Metropolis! In the insanity of the last half hour, Lois hadn't realized that it, too, could have been damaged — or destroyed — in the bombardment.

She closed her eyes and thought, *Thank heavens for Superman!*

She glanced down at her watch. "Too late to make the evening edition! Metropolis will have to wait till morning to read about this particular exploit." She grinned up at Superman. "I'd like to see Clark Kent top this story!"

They climbed the steps into the half-destroyed reception building. Superman lifted the concrete slab and retrieved her purse.

Then they strolled out into the crisp autumn air. A full moon shone down on them. Trees tossed in a light breeze.

At first glance, Lois thought her car looked drivable, if a bit dented. Then she saw the ragged hole punched through the hood.

She checked the engine. A fist-sized meteorite was embedded there.

Superman pulled out the rock and offered it to her. "A souvenir, Lois? Of your Cadmus adventure?"

Lois took it. "My own little chunk of starlight." She

gave him a crooked smile. "I guess this is what I have insurance for. Want to give a girl a ride?"

"Home?" he asked her.

"No way!" She grinned. "I need to write this up!"

Superman scooped Lois up. Still clutching her souvenir meteorite, she wrapped her arms around his neck. Then he leaped into the sky.

Wind whipped Lois's curls as they rose above the treetops. He felt her hair brush his cheek and tangle around his hand. She smelled of honeysuckle . . . and dust.

For a moment, he hovered with her in the moonlight, looking down at Project Cadmus. From this vantage point, the damage was obvious. Downed trees, smashed outbuildings and fences. Small-impact craters. And several holes plowed into the side of the mountain.

"It's a huge operation," Lois murmured. "I wonder what they're up to."

"No good, probably," he joked. He started to ask her if she'd gotten an answer about the space signal, then stopped. It was Clark, not Superman, who knew about that.

He sighed. It was one more small, depressing example of why he hated keeping his dual identity a secret from her.

Why should I bother with a Clark Kent identity at all? he thought suddenly. As Superman he had Lois, the woman he loved, in his arms. As Clark he had — What? A pal? A rival?

I hate leading a double life, he thought. *Being on guard. Worrying about what I say and do, so I don't accidentally give myself away. If I lived my life as Superman alone, I wouldn't have to live a lie.*

He held Lois close — safe and warm — and carried her toward Metropolis.

Several floors below, Project Cadmus personnel found Dr. Emmet Vale beneath a slab of concrete. He was barely conscious, but his arm was outstretched, his hand convulsively clutching a chunk of meteorite that glowed an eerie green. He could no longer move his body.

They rushed Vale many floors below, to the Cadmus

in-house medical facility. Machines kept him alive while tests confirmed that his back had been badly broken near the top of his spine. The damage was irreversible and devastating.

When they gave him the news, Vale smiled and whispered, "I'll have a new body . . . a better body. Put my brain . . . into Metallo."

Vale's chief assistant was appalled. "We can't put your brain in that metal monstrosity," he said. "Your mind's too valuable. What if something goes wrong?"

"Already . . . gone wrong," Vale whispered. "And now . . . gone right. Who better to test Metallo . . . than the designer?"

"What about the power problem?" the assistant countered. "You said that without an adequate and continuous power supply, Metallo can't operate at full capability."

"Power supply . . . on the table," Vale murmured. His eyes shifted to the meteorite he had been clutching when the ceiling crashed down on top of him.

"Kryptonite!" Vale whispered. "I'll destroy Superman . . . with kryptonite."

Lois stared at the city glittering with lights. Then she looked up into Superman's face.

He protected all that, she thought. *He's so handsome. So good. So perfect. And right now, he's about a million miles away.*

"Where do you go?" she asked him suddenly.

He looked down at her. "Go?"

"I mean . . . when you aren't fighting off meteors and saving the world," she explained, suddenly flustered. She hadn't meant to ask him that out loud.

He smiled crookedly. "Lois, is this an interview?"

"N-no," she stammered. "Not . . . not really. It's just . . . I was thinking. You have all that power. But you have compassion for people, too. And humanity. It makes me think you don't spend your downtime in an ivory tower. It makes me wonder. . . ."

Superman thought about his Fortress of Solitude — a towering, cathedral-like structure in the Arctic, grown from a Kryptonian Master Crystal. It was wondrous. But it was also cold and lonely.

"Crystal," he said. "My tower isn't ivory. It's crystal . . . and ice."

Suddenly, the Daily Planet globe was below them. *Much too soon,* he thought. He didn't want to let her go.

He sank toward the rooftop slowly, settled beneath the spinning globe, and stood there with Lois in his arms.

"We're here," she said. "Thank you!"

He smiled down at her. "For what?"

"For giving me a lift. And for saving my life." She leaned up and kissed him softly. Then she slid to the ground.

"My pleasure," he said. He bent down and kissed her again. *She's what I want,* he thought.

When he stepped back, she asked, "Where are you going now?"

Superman grinned. "Up into the sunlight to recharge my batteries. Then to check the outskirts of Metropolis. As you saw, I wasn't able to stop all the meteors. There may be people who need my help."

She smiled and backed away, then watched as he raced into the air — higher and higher until, in seconds, he was gone.

She gazed down at the meteorite still clutched in her hand. It had been a strange day . . . but it seemed to have had a very happy ending.

She walked toward the access door and down the stairs to the elevators.

She had a story to write — one that would knock Perry's socks off.

6

"What? No pictures?" Perry White asked the next morning.

Lois, arms folded, stood before his massive desk and fumed.

"Olsen!" Perry White swung his chair and looked at Jimmy accusingly. "Why weren't you with Lane?"

"Uh . . . ," Jimmy stalled.

Perry scowled. "Where Lane goes, Superman goes . . . or so it seems! So you stick to her like glue!" He glared at Jimmy. "From now on, you're her shadow!"

"Really?" Jimmy grinned like a maniac. "Thanks, Chief!"

"But, Chief —" Lois began. She realized Perry had a point. She also knew if Jimmy was along, she could kiss her love life, such as it was, good-bye. The last

thing she and Superman needed was a chaperone —
especially one with a camera.

Perry frowned at Lois. "Where's Superman now?"

Lois huffed. "How should I know? It's not like he
leaves me a schedule."

"He's in Rome. Or he was a few minutes ago," Jimmy
said. The others looked at him questioningly. Jimmy
shrugged. "Some terrorist threat to the Coliseum. It's
on the news. International feed."

At that, Perry smiled warmly. "My nephew, Richard,
has been hired to take over the international division
here at the *Planet*," he announced. "He's in Rome now!"

"Swell! Maybe he can get you a picture!" Lois's
mood was still sour. "He any good?"

Perry smiled proudly. "Chip off the old block! In
other words, he's brilliant!"

Lois rolled her eyes.

When he awoke on the operating table in the Project
Cadmus robotics lab, he was no longer Emmet Vale. He

was Metallo . . . and he had acquired power beyond his wildest dreams.

He sat up, noting how well the metal body responded to his mental command. It was attached to wires that ran to machines measuring his responses and feeding information to computers assigned to monitor him.

He could feel the power of kryptonite pulsing in his metal chest.

"Excellent," he said to his team of human assistants. His voice was toneless, robotic. He was glad now that they had run when the roof buckled. He had needed them alive and well to perform this transfer.

He shifted his head to study each of them in turn, and saw them take a step back.

They were afraid of him, he realized. Of the power he had acquired. Of what he had become. They were right to be.

He stretched out a gleaming silver hand, made a fist, and brought it down hard on the beeping machine that measured his brain waves. Its metal casing broke, and its innards shattered into a thousand tiny pieces.

Invulnerability and superstrength, he thought. *What other powers do I have now?*

He concentrated then, feeling the pulses of knowledge running to and from the other machines. One by one, he took control of them.

For the moment, he would leave them attached. It would give the Cadmus bigwigs the illusion of control. But the wires were two-way conduits. They gave him access to Project Cadmus's computers. He would learn everything they knew.

And then he would take over Cadmus . . . and destroy Superman.

∞　　∞　　∞

Lois drove the rental car up the mountain road.

She had left Jimmy behind at the *Planet*. She had assured him she wasn't going after a story, just taking personal time to arrange to have her car towed to a repair shop.

She didn't mention that her car had been in the Cadmus parking lot. Or that she had rescheduled her appointment to interview Dr. Welles concerning the space signal.

She rationalized this omission by telling herself that Perry wanted pictures of Superman. And since Superman was in Europe, Jimmy's traveling with her to Cadmus would benefit no one.

Lois drove up to the guardhouse and noted, with surprise, that it had already been repaired. Once again, a guard took her ID, a bit mangled from having been in her crushed purse, and checked it, along with her appointment.

Fifteen seconds later, he returned it to her and directed her to the same visitor parking space as yesterday's, telling her that Dr. Welles would be waiting. She smiled, certain that because of the damage to the exterior building, she would once again be allowed into the hidden Cadmus.

As she parked, that hope was dashed. The windowless visitor's area, like the guardhouse, had already been repaired.

So much for my brilliant plan to get inside and find out

what they're up to, she thought. *This organization is so efficient, it's beginning to creep me out.*

Deep in the bowels of Project Cadmus, Metallo lay on his gurney. The machines connected to his brain and metal body registered sleep patterns for anyone who might be checking on his condition. Those were the patterns Metallo wanted them to see.

Metallo had moved beyond controlling those machines to exploring other facets of Cadmus now open to him. He closed his mind to outside stimulus and interfaced with the Cadmus computer equipment.

He was fascinated to discover just how carefully the Cadmus personnel were watched. Bugs and cameras were everywhere.

Quite a paranoid crew we have running this place, he thought. If he'd had lips, he would have smiled.

He interfaced with the cameras, watching as workers moved about the complex.

He registered Lois Lane's press ID as it was checked through the scanner.

What's the Lane woman doing here again? he wondered. *You'd think yesterday would have taught her to keep away from where she wasn't wanted.*

He checked and saw that she had rescheduled her interview with Dr. Welles. Welles was a radio astronomer. What did the Lane woman want with him?

Metallo mentally shrugged. Finding out would be child's play. All he had to do was watch the interview.

❦   ❦   ❦

Dr. Stanford Welles was a slight, dark-haired man with large brown eyes and an enthusiastic manner. He shook Lois's hand and sat with her in the interview room.

"The signal is real," he told her. "Picked up by the *Starfarer* satellite and relayed back to Earth. It's from the sector of space where the planet Krypton's sun went nova. *National Scientific* magazine will be running an article on it next month.

"We know that Superman came from Krypton. And I think it is very likely we are hearing a distress call from other survivors."

Other Kryptonians! Metallo thought, as he watched through a camera's lens as Lois Lane drove away. *I was right! Superman is just the spearhead, softening Earth up for an invasion of alien superbeings!*

He would have to destroy Superman soon, before the alien could find these beings and lead an attack on the earth. But destroying Superman would take more than power. Metallo would also need a plan.

He considered Lois Lane. She had been in the tunnel with Superman when the roof caved in on him.

He reviewed the tapes of Superman trying to hold up the ceiling, then falling — brought low by the kryptonite in the meteorite.

Another tape showed the Lane woman dragging Superman away from the kryptonite toward safety, the roof collapsing, and Superman sheltering her with his own body.

Metallo studied their interaction as Lane and Superman walked together through the Cadmus corridors. And as Superman flew away with her in his arms.

She's the main chronicler of his adventures, his friend, and possibly his lover, Metallo decided. *Lois Lane is the key. Superman makes a habit of coming to her rescue. All I have to do is have her kidnapped and Superman will follow . . . and fall into my trap.*

In preparation, he shifted his attention to the nano-construct, Bizarro.

More Kryptonian survivors! Lois mused, as she passed the guardhouse and began her drive down the mountain. *But their planet was utterly destroyed. How is that possible?*

Should I tell Superman? Tell him that maybe — probably — he isn't really the last of his kind. That others like him are out there. And that possibly they're in trouble.

As she slowed at the turnoff to the repair shop, her mind was in turmoil.

If I tell him, maybe he'll leave to find them. And if I don't, she realized with dismay, *the* National Scientific *article will come out and he'll find out anyway.*

But is it accurate?

She had no reason to think Dr. Stanford Welles was

lying, but something about him just didn't ring true. Maybe it was simply the unnatural willingness of any Cadmus employee to speak to her about anything at all.

I'll check out the National Scientific *data and Dr. Welles's credentials first,* she decided. *If they pan out, I'll have to tell Superman.*

And if they don't, she thought grimly, *then somebody's going to a lot of trouble to get Superman out of town.*

It was the middle of the night when the robot Metallo strode into the laboratory where the Superman clone, Bizarro, floated in his vat, not yet awakened.

Earlier, Metallo had checked the Cadmus spy monitors. The night guards were huddled around their computer screens or immersed in other tasks. As long as he didn't trip any alarms, no one would bother with him.

Nevertheless, Metallo ordered the cameras that observed him to show steady images of his robot body lying peacefully on his gurney. It was easy to create loops in the recordings so there would be no visual or audio record of his movements around Cadmus.

Or of the event that would soon take place in this laboratory.

Metallo stalked toward the vat, where the naked, chalk-white figure floated in its vat of clear fluid.

For a moment he studied the angular, slablike face with its shock of straight dark hair.

Wires ran to implants in the creature's skull. Some were used to teach language and basic human behavior. Others fed him virtual-reality simulations of Superman's exploits, as if they were his own.

Brain implants stimulated the portions of his brain that controlled his superpowers. Other electrodes on his body caused his muscles to contract and release as he dreamed his manufactured dreams.

In these simulations, Bizarro was, and always had been, the one and only Superman.

Since Lois had left Cadmus that afternoon, Metallo had taken over Bizarro's controls and begun the creature's final programming.

He had introduced Lois Lane into Bizarro's dreamworld.

Again and again, Bizarro rescued his true love from

the danger posed by a false Superman and carried her to Cadmus, where she would be safe. And each time Metallo, Bizarro's creator, was waiting to destroy the pretender.

Metallo inserted the tip of his index finger into a USB port and interfaced with the computers and machinery that encouraged Bizarro's development and kept him alive.

One by one, he withdrew most of the wires and electrodes from Bizarro's brain and body. Then he drained the tank.

As the liquid flowed out, Bizarro settled to the bottom of the tank. He stood upright on his own two feet.

A good sign. Metallo silently rejoiced.

Metallo sent a jolt of energy through the remaining wires into Bizarro's brain and heart. "Wake up!" he commanded the creature. "Breathe!"

The creature's chest rose . . . and fell . . . once . . . twice . . . and Bizarro opened his eyes.

7

The next morning, Superman returned to Metropolis from Rome. As he flew overhead, people on the streets waved and smiled. Others shouted their thanks and approval. Superman grinned and waved back.

Lois's article must have been pretty amazing to create that kind of reaction, he thought. *I guess not everyone in Metropolis thinks I'm an alien monster!*

Superman frowned.

Where had that sudden bitterness come from? He'd run across the occasional human before who saw him as different and therefore frightening. And mostly, he'd shrugged it off, figuring it was their problem.

What made that Cadmus scientist, Vale, any different?

The rest of Metropolis is glad I had the power to stop those meteors, he told himself. *They aren't worrying about where the power came from. I should just be happy I could help.*

Except Vale hadn't wanted his help. He had been willing to stand there and let the ceiling fall on him rather than accept Superman's aid.

Just the thought of Vale made his stomach churn. He felt anxious and unsettled.

What was the matter with him, anyway?

⚉   ⚉   ⚉

That morning, Lois rushed into the Planet bullpen, scribbled her notes about the alleged signals from outer space, and stuck them in a folder among all the other folders piled on her desk. Then she made an appointment to meet with the arson investigator at Grimbly's Department Store about the fire.

She was dashing toward the bullpen doors when Jimmy Olsen pushed his way in. "Hi, Miss Lane! Where are you —?"

"Later, Jimmy. I'm running late," Lois tried to explain as she dashed for the elevator. She knew Perry had said to take Jimmy with her and that she shouldn't have brushed the kid off.

I'll make it up to him, she told herself. *But right now, I have to hurry.*

In the elevator she glanced around. All morning she'd had the oddest feeling that she was being watched.

Enough is enough, Jimmy decided. Perry had told him to stick with Lois and he was going to do that — whether she wanted him to or not.

He already had his camera with him, so he turned and sprinted after her. As he burst through the bullpen doors into the hall, the elevator doors were closing. *Darn!*

He raced for the stairwell.

Fifteen flights later, he pushed open the exit door, ran into the lobby, barreled through the brass-trimmed lobby doors, and looked around, panting.

Midmorning traffic was practically at a standstill. If Miss Lane had grabbed a cab, she couldn't have gone far.

Then Jimmy spotted her disappearing down the steps to the subway.

As he followed her, he felt in his pocket for his MetropoCard. He swiped it through the turnstile just as the subway train roared into the station.

Late rush hour commuters hurried past while Jimmy craned his neck, searching for Lois. He spotted her down the platform. He knew he wouldn't have time to reach her.

So he shoved his way into the crowded subway car right in front of him, standing next to the door where he could look out and, he hoped, spot Lois when she left the train.

He traveled one stop . . . two . . . three stops, popping his head out like a jack-in-the-box each time to look for her. The fourth platform was bustling, so by the time he spotted her, the doors to his car were closing.

He shoved the metal doors back open. A warning alarm buzzed and the doors bruised his arms. But he shouldered his way out, onto the jam-packed platform.

He pushed through the crowd, wondering where Lois was going, trying to keep her in sight.

It was close to eleven when Clark Kent walked through the swinging doors into the bustling Daily Planet bullpen.

He'd been to his apartment, gotten his mail, and checked the newspapers tossed on the table beneath his mailbox. Clark grinned, remembering yesterday's headline: SAVIOR OF METROPOLIS. No wonder people had greeted him like he'd risen from the dead.

His own article on meteor damage to the outer suburbs had been relegated to page three. *Guess you can't win 'em all,* he thought.

A quick shower, clean clothes, and he'd been good to go.

Now he glanced toward Lois's messy desk, planning to congratulate her. She wasn't there. Jimmy didn't seem to be around, either.

Lois was out, then, following up on some story or other, and had finally agreed to take Jimmy with her. She probably wasn't up to anything dangerous since he didn't hear alarms or sirens anywhere in the city. In fact, Metropolis seemed almost unnaturally peaceful.

Clark figured he'd take the downtime to follow up on a few stories himself.

Lois was hurrying through the busy streets toward Grimbly's Department Store when, once again, she felt strange eyes upon her.

She looked left and right, then up.

High above Metropolis, a figure hovered, silhouetted against the bright, mid-morning sky. His red cape waved like a flag in the wind.

It's Superman, she told herself. *He's back in Metropolis.* She waved up at him and he waved back.

But the odd, slightly creeped-out feeling didn't go away.

"Miss Lane," a strained voice said behind her. A hand gripped her arm.

Lois whirled, startled. "Jimmy, what are you —?" Then she was grabbed around the waist and snatched up into the sky.

"Do not worry, Lois Lane," a deep but somehow childlike voice said in her ear. "Superman am here to save you!"

She watched the ground recede quickly . . . then turned her head and looked into the face of a monster.

Out of the corner of her eye, Lois caught a flash as Jimmy Olsen's camera went off down below.

"Who are you?" she asked in a strangled voice, trying not to panic.

"Me am Superman!" the monster said. He sounded surprised she'd asked.

Riiiiight, Lois thought. She studied her captor.

His forehead was high and square, jutting out over his dark eyes. His face was sharply angled, as if it had been roughly chipped from stone. His skin was very white and had a rocklike sheen. His black hair was long and uneven.

His frame was large boned. *His hands are huge,* she noted. But they held her gently.

He was wearing a skintight blue suit, red boots, and a red cape. He had an S-shield on his chest.

The creature *did* seem to think he was Superman.

And he had, at least, Superman's power of flight. She was tempted to try to set him straight, but she realized that eight stories in the air was no place to argue.

"You know who I am?" she asked, playing for time.

"You am reporter for *Daily Planet* newspaper. You write stories about Superman. Superman love you. And you love Superman. Why you not know who you am? You always know that before."

Yes, Superman loves me, she thought. *And I love him. But who knows about our relationship? We've been so careful.*

Wait a minute. He said . . .

"Before . . . ?" Lois asked.

"Whenever me save you," he explained patiently. "Lois, did bad-man-who-pretend-to-be-Superman knock you on head?"

Lois looked down. They had risen to the top of the highest skyscrapers. She didn't want to get the monster upset. She definitely didn't want him to drop her.

Knowledge is power, she thought. *The best way to find out what's happening is to keep him talking.*

"Where are you taking me?" she asked as the monster turned northwest.

"To place me go. Superman's place."

Just a few days ago, she had asked Superman — the real Superman — where he went. He had talked about a tower of crystal and ice . . .

"What kind of place?"

Bizarro screwed up his face in thought. "Am called mountain," he said. "Am also called . . . Superman doesn't know name."

"Why are you taking me there?"

"Me am keeping you safe. Bad-man-who-pretend-to-be-Superman will come and . . . and try hurt you." Bizarro frowned as the fantasy simulation played out in his mind. There were some dark images of the other Superman dying at the end. Finally he said, "Metallo will kill bad man. But . . . me not like killing." He sounded confused.

Lois glanced down. They were still flying northwest, above the run-down section of Metropolis called Suicide Slum. "Who's Metallo?" she asked.

"He . . . it —" Bizarro frowned down at her. "This not happening way it should. You not supposed to ask questions."

"You said I'm a reporter, right? So it's my job to ask questions, isn't it?"

Oddly enough, Lois felt herself losing her fear of her captor. Whatever was happening, she was beginning to think it wasn't this creature's fault.

8

Jimmy dashed into the Daily Planet bullpen clutching his camera like a prize. His face was red. His hair was sticking out wildly. He looked like he had run a marathon.

The young photographer stumbled into Perry White's office, babbling excitedly. "It's Miss Lane, Chief. She's been —"

But Perry wasn't there. Jimmy looked around wildly.

"Jimmy, what is it?"

Jimmy turned and saw Clark. "A large white monster wearing a Superman suit flew in and grabbed Miss Lane. I . . . I got pictures. I called the cops but they said —"

Clark grabbed Jimmy's shoulders. "Where did it take her?"

"Northwest," Jimmy gasped. "Toward Suicide Slum."

Lois looked up at the creature that held her gently in his arms. The streets of Suicide Slum slipped past below.

He doesn't seem too bright, Lois thought. *But I don't think he's one of the bad guys. Maybe I can reason with him.*

"So this Metallo guy sent you to get me because he wanted Superman — I mean the bad-man-who-pretends-to-be-Superman — to follow you to the mountain?" she asked.

Bizarro frowned, concentrating hard. "That right."

"The problem is — the Metallo guy tricked you. The other Superman isn't a bad guy. He's the real Superman. You're . . ." Lois wasn't sure what he was — some kind of bizarre clone or construct, maybe.

"No," Bizarro insisted. "*Me* real Superman. Me prove it. Me show you heat vision!"

"Don't!" Lois cried. But it was too late.

Red beams shot from Bizarro's eyes.

PZAPT! The beams struck an old, empty water tower on top of a deserted factory building.

CRACK! The water tower broke loose and tumbled toward the crowded sidewalk.

"No!" Bizarro cried. "Superman not hurt people. Me save them!"

Lois felt the g-force as Bizarro dived. Inches above the heads of the startled pedestrians, he tackled the falling tower with an outstretched arm. But he was going too fast to stop.

Bizarro, Lois, and the water tower plowed through the wall and into the abandoned building.

Sheltered by Bizarro's invulnerable body, Lois was protected from the impact and from the broken water tower, which shattered into pieces around her.

They smashed through a concrete floor and crashed onto the landing below. She lay sprawled half on top of Bizarro, trying to get her breath.

"Me not mean that to happen," the bizarre-Superman muttered. "That never happen before."

Lois realized that her captor seemed concerned that events were unfolding differently from the way they were supposed to happen, the way he thought he remembered them happening. Maybe that was the key.

77

"Listen, why don't you tell me about the times be—" she began.

CRACK! CRACK! CRACK!

At the ominous sounds, she froze. "What's that?"

The building shuddered. She squinted through the interior darkness toward the hole her kidnapper had bashed in the wall and floor.

Outside, voices were screaming.

"Run!"

"The front of the building!"

"It's coming down!"

∞ ∞ ∞

Like a speeding bullet, Superman flew toward Suicide Slum. All his supersenses were alert. He kept checking the distance with telescopic vision, hoping for a glimpse of Lois and her kidnapper. He listened for any disturbance with his superhearing.

He was past Suicide Slum, over the West River, and nearly to Queensland Park when he heard the cracking sound followed by screams.

He doubled back toward Suicide Slum, scanning for the source of the noise with X-ray and telescopic vision.

He spotted it. Part of the brick façade of an old factory building had begun to give way. Debris was starting to cascade down its front like an avalanche. Pedestrians were running, but not all of them would escape the rock fall. And there were too many slow ones for Superman to scoop them all to safety.

Superman spotted a big green metal Dumpster across the street from the factory. Moving at superspeed, he snatched it up and flew, holding it overhead to catch the falling debris.

Bricks and slabs of concrete thudded into the Dumpster with a sound like rolling thunder. In seconds, the Dumpster was overflowing.

Beneath the shelter of the Dumpster, two young boys with a basketball, a crippled panhandler, a woman pushing a stroller, and a blind old man and the teenager who was helping him huddled unharmed as bricks slid off the pile and crashed onto the street beyond them.

Through the hole in the wall, Lois had seen the bricks beginning to fall. And then there was Superman. For a second she watched him hover beside the hole, holding something large overhead.

Then came a deafening clatter and he sank from sight.

Lois turned to her kidnapper. "That's Superman," she shouted above the racket. "The *real* Superman. *You* knocked the hole in the wall and made those bricks fall. And the real Superman came and kept them from hurting people. Somebody has tricked you into thinking you're him!"

"No!" Her captor leaped to his feet. "Me am real Superman! *Me* save people, too! Me can fly! Me have heat vision!"

"So does he!" Lois argued.

"No! Me save you! You see!" He looked around desperately. The falling bricks had torn away the boards that covered one of the windows.

Bizarro snatched Lois into his arms and leaped through the window and into the sky.

♾ ♾ ♾

Superman began to lower the Dumpster to the street. Suddenly a being who looked like he'd been chipped from marble flew out a window of the abandoned factory. He was wearing a blue bodysuit and a red cape, much like Superman's. And he was holding Lois in his arms.

KLANG! Superman set the Dumpster onto the street and was after him like a shot.

He tackled the monster in midflight and dragged him down toward the ground.

Bizarro wrenched one leg free and kicked Superman in the shoulder, sending him hurtling backward.

Whoever — whatever — he is, he's as strong as I am, Superman realized grimly. *But maybe he's not quite as fast.*

Pulling back his arm, Superman zipped in front of the monster. He slammed a fist hard into its jaw.

The monster jerked backward, its grip on Lois loosened, and Superman swept her into his arms.

The monster fell back and down through the roof of a parked car.

"No! Don't hurt him!" Lois cried to Superman. "He's not really dangerous!"

Superman looked at her like she'd lost her mind.

"Or at least, he doesn't mean to be," she explained. "He thinks he's —"

"He's what?" Superman snapped through gritted teeth. Lois had never seen him look so furious. "My evil twin Skippy?"

Lois frowned at him in exasperation. "I think he's some sort of construct. Someone made him and dressed him like that. They convinced him somehow that he's you! He thinks I'm his —"

Down below, Bizarro struggled into the air.

"Bad man not hurt my Lois!" he shouted. "Me save you!" The creature picked up a parked delivery van, swung it overhead, and hurled it at Superman.

Then the creature raced toward them, intent on snatching Lois from Superman's arms.

"Is that how you save her?" Superman snarled as he caught the van's fender. "By throwing a car at her? By endangering other people? That's not how Superman acts!"

When Bizarro bulleted in, Superman kicked out with his foot, catching the monster beneath its chin, sending it spinning out over the West River.

As Superman turned to fly after it, the metal fender of the van ripped away. The van began to fall.

Still holding Lois in one arm, Superman dove past the van, came up under its body, and caught it by an axel before it could crash through the roof of a brownstone.

He swooped to the ground, released Lois, and lowered the van onto the street.

Only then did he leap skyward again.

He hovered, looking around for the monster. But it was gone.

9

"You think someone made him?" Superman growled through gritted teeth, as he carried Lois toward the Daily Planet building. "Why?"

"Because he isn't natural!" Lois rolled her eyes. Superman wasn't usually this dense. But, then, she had never seen him so angry. "Someone named Metallo wanted to use him and me like bait, to lure you into a trap. This Metallo plans to kill you."

"Then why didn't that . . . monster wait around?" Superman demanded. "Why did he just disappear?"

Lois hesitated. "I don't know. He seemed confused. . . ."

Superman frowned at her. "You feel sorry for that thing, don't you?"

"Of course I do. Imagine what it would be like to think you were one thing, but you were really something else," she said. "What it would be like to live a lie! He's trying so hard to be Superman."

That one hit home with Superman. "You think that . . . monster is like me?" he asked.

"That's not what I said." *Honestly, it's almost like he wants to pick a fight,* Lois thought to herself. "He's not you. He's nothing like you beyond the powers someone gave him and the suit he's wearing."

Except . . . she thought. *His gentleness. His bravery. His determination to help. Whoever made the monster got those parts right.*

"I just don't think any of it's his fault!" she finished lamely.

Superman scowled down at the Daily Planet globe. "I can't believe someone created that twisted doppelgänger. You saw the mess he made of that building. What if people think I —?"

"Nobody who saw him would even begin to think that he was you," Lois soothed.

As Superman landed with her on the roof of the Daily Planet building, he growled, "I'm going to scour this town until I find him. And the guy who made him."

Which is exactly what Metallo wants, Lois thought. She looked northwest and thought about Cadmus.

⚬⚬   ⚬⚬   ⚬⚬

"Now *this* will sell papers! You see how much better the story will be with a picture?" Perry White handed Lois Jimmy's series of shots. "Now aren't you glad I made you take Jimmy with you?"

Lois glanced at the photos, then over at Jimmy, who was busily photocopying, head down, not looking at them.

So Jimmy hadn't told Perry she'd tried to ditch him. He'd used his initiative and gotten great shots of Bizarro carrying her off . . . and now he was worried he'd done something wrong. *I'm the one who ought to be ashamed,* Lois told herself.

"Hey, Jimmy. Nice photos," she called over to him. "I'll let you know when I go out again!"

86

Jimmy looked startled, then grinned broadly. "Thanks, Miss Lane," he called back. "I always said you were the best! You and Mr. Kent! I'm just glad Superman got there in time to save you!"

Superman was too unsettled, too angry and restless, to go back to work.

Instead, he flew home to the farm in Kansas to visit his mother. He did this often. His father — his human father — had died a while back, and he knew she got lonely.

He sat at the kitchen table and told her everything. The meteors. The cave-in at Cadmus. The weird scientist, Dr. Vale, who would rather die than accept help from an alien monster.

Then he told her about the hideous doppelgänger that kidnapped Lois, hoping to lure him to his death.

"I can't believe somebody tried to make a clone of me," he stormed. "And the duplicate they made was a monster! Do they really see me like that?"

"A few, probably." Martha Kent frowned. "The rest know you for the decent man you are. There are laws against cloning humans, son. And rightly so."

Superman shrugged angrily. "The point is, I'm *not* human. Things keep piling up on me these days, *reminding* me."

Martha bit her lip. "Most people are good at heart. But there are always a few rotten apples in the barrel." She sighed. "This is the sort of craziness Jonathan and I worried about. It's one of the reasons we kept your true origin a secret."

⊷   ⊷   ⊷

"Hey, Miss Lane, listen to this," Jimmy Olsen said excitedly.

Lois looked up from the Grimbly's story she was writing. Jimmy was taking his assignment as her photographer very seriously. On his lunch hour, he'd even gone out to buy a radio that would let him eavesdrop on police transmissions in case she needed story ideas.

At first Lois had found his enthusiasm endearing.

But after an afternoon filled with "Listen to this!" she decided it just might drive her around the bend.

"What?" She could hear the exasperation in her voice.

"It sounds like that Superman doppelgänger is back," Jimmy said. "A barge just slammed into the houseboats at the 79th Street Boat Basin. The doppelgänger is trying to sort it out."

She leaped to her feet.

"C'mon, partner!" she said. "This I've gotta see!"

⚭   ⚭   ⚭

Superman flew over the Arctic snow and ice, over whales, seals, and polar bears. The aurora borealis shimmered overhead, a curtain of multicolored light.

He entered the cloudlike vortex that swirled over the Fortress of Solitude and protected it from the eyes of prying satellites.

In seconds, he landed before the towering crystalline Fortress. He entered the vaulting main chamber and ran his hand over the smooth top of the central console.

Within the console, lights flared. Some crystals rose

from the top, others fell, creating indentations in its surface. At the center of the console, the foot-long Master Crystal rose highest and glowed brightest of all.

The Master Crystal, sent by Jor-El in the rocket that had brought his infant son to Earth, had created the great Fortress, but it had other purposes as well.

Among its many wonders, the Master Crystal was loaded with three-dimensional interactive images of his father and mother and the keys to a Kryptonian science so advanced that it seemed like magic.

Superman picked up the Master Crystal and placed it into the largest hole in the console.

Shafts of light illuminated the Fortress, and the huge crystals sparkled like diamonds.

Then whispers echoed all around him. And within the crystal walls, multiple images of a white-haired man in a long tunic appeared. He said, "My son."

Just as Superman had told his human mother what had happened, now he told his Kryptonian father, Jor-El.

". . . a doppelgänger, white as if it had been carved of alabaster marble. But alive . . . and monstrous. Is this how they see me? Is it what I truly am?"

"Some of them will look at you and see only your power. They will be jealous or fearful. After all, the earth's yellow sun gives you the ability to blast whoever displeases you into dust."

Superman scowled. "I couldn't do that. I wouldn't!"

"Those who fear and hate you most are the ones who would misuse the power if it were theirs," Jor-El said. "They judge you by how they judge themselves."

"I'm tired of being different," Superman muttered. "Of watching what I say and do. Of always being careful. Would it be so wrong to live among them openly, as I am?"

Jor-El shook his head sadly. "You can live among the people of Earth in any way you choose, my son, but you must accept what your choice will mean. As you must also accept that you can never truly be like them. You are something . . . special. As humanity has adopted and protected you, in time you will save them —"

"I don't want to be their savior! I want to be —" Superman snapped. He was thinking about Lois. "This . . . difference puts a wall around me that I don't know how to break through. To live as one of them is to live a lie. To live without them is to condemn myself to even greater isolation."

"This is a very real problem and one that you will have to grapple with," his father said. "But you are still young, my son. In time, you'll find the balance you seek."

10

Jimmy and Lois stood on the 79th Street overlook, staring down in amazement at the marina below.

Normally, the seven wooden piers of the Boat Basin jutted out serenely into the West River, creating moorings for houseboats and small cabin cruisers. Several yachts were always anchored farther out, in a deeper channel.

Now, a garbage barge that had somehow broken loose from the tugboat towing it downriver had slammed into the center of the marina. The impact had splintered the central pier and driven houseboats into one another. Several had sprung leaks and, despite the desperate bailing of their occupants, were beginning to sink.

The Superman doppelgänger hovered over the chaos, looking confused.

As Lois and Jimmy watched, Bizarro lifted one end of the barge, apparently hoping to free it from the wreckage.

But several of the houseboats, whose mooring lines had become entangled with the barge, were pulled partway into the air with it. A layer of smelly garbage spilled from the barge into the water.

Police helicopters swarmed, tugboats chugged up the river, and the owners of the houseboats yelled angrily.

"Me am Superman! Me am fixing boats and saving people," Bizarro grumbled loudly. "Why boats not cooperate? Why people get so mad?"

"Where's Superman? Why isn't he here?" Jimmy muttered. "I've got tons of shots of this clown and not one shot of Superman!"

Out over the marina, Bizarro gave another tug on the barge, trying to drag it backward. A sharp corner of the barge ripped across a houseboat, tearing a deep gash in its side.

That houseboat, too, began to sink.

Lois had felt the urge to laugh at first, but not anymore. Those houseboats were people's homes, their creative solution to the lack of affordable apartments in Metropolis. And one by one, they were being demolished.

Jimmy snapped picture after picture.

"I've got to get closer," he muttered to Lois. During a lull in the action, he sprinted down the steps toward the marina.

Bizarro let go of the barge. He flew over to the gashed houseboat and tried to lift it to safety but it was still tied to the dock.

Red beams slashed from Bizarro's eyes as he used heat vision to sever the mooring rope. The rope snapped apart, but the pier beyond it burst into flame.

As Bizarro jerked the houseboat into the air, gasoline splashed from its damaged fuel tank onto the pier, the water, and several other houseboats below.

WHUMPH! Houseboats, pier, and water's surface all ignited.

"Abandon ship!" someone shouted. "Run!"

People dove from burning houseboats into the water.

Out on the river, the yachts and cabin cruisers began to pull away fast. Houseboats moored to the undamaged piers began to rev their engines.

The doppelgänger hovered, looking distraught. Lois could see that he couldn't understand how all of this had happened. And that he didn't know what to do next.

They needed Superman — the real Superman — but he wasn't there.

I have to do something, Lois thought. *Fast, before the whole Boat Basin goes up in flames.* She remembered the fire at Grimbly's and how Superman had put it out.

"Superman," she shouted, hoping the doppelgänger had the rest of Superman's powers, especially superhearing.

Bizarro's head came up. He looked right at her. She saw his mouth shape the word, "Lois!"

"Use superbreath," she shouted.

Bizarro looked back at the fire. It was spreading rapidly. Soon it would be out of control.

He took a huge breath . . . and blew.

With a *WHUMPH!* the blaze went out.

Lois could see him practically sag with relief.

"Now get away from there," she called. She pointed toward the roof of a high-rise apartment building on the edge of West River Park. "Wait for me. Up there. Let the tugboats and police take it from here!"

Bizarro flew off, leaving charred confusion in his wake.

Lois rushed down the steps to the smoldering pier, where Jimmy was still snapping pictures. "Jimmy, when you're done here, go back to the *Planet* and get your shots developed. With any luck, we'll make the evening edition."

Jimmy looked at her startled. "Me? Where are *you* going?"

"I need to do a quick interview. I shouldn't be long," she said. Before Jimmy could argue, she dashed up the steps and out of his sight.

Minutes later, she ducked into the alley beside the high-rise.

"Hey, Superman!" she called. "Down here!"

Bizarro dropped down in front of her. "Not Superman," he said. "Superman save people, but me make fire. Lois am right. Me am not Superman. Me am . . . something else. Men on boats say me monster!"

"You aren't Superman, but you aren't a monster either," she told him gently. "You tried to help, but using superpowers properly is hard." And as she said it, she thought that until now she'd never realized just how hard it must be. Superman always made it look so easy.

"I know one way we can find out what you are, though," she told him. "Take me to Metallo . . . and we'll ask him together."

⚭   ⚭   ⚭

Jimmy rushed from the developing room into the Daily Planet bullpen with a sheaf of photos clutched in his hand.

Clark was stomping down the center aisle ahead of him, muttering to himself. He tossed a *Metropolis Times* down on his desk.

Jimmy glanced at the *Times,* wondering what Mr. Kent was doing with a rival paper, and read the headline: SUPERMAN OR SUPERMENACE? Below the headline was a blurry shot of a caped figure lifting a van over his head.

"Can't they tell the difference between Superman and that . . . that monster?" Clark muttered.

Jimmy studied the photo with professional interest.

"Probably not from that distance. Heck, that could be anybody standing there," Jimmy said scornfully. "Must've been taken with a telephoto lens from half a mile away. The shots I got tonight at the Boat Basin are way better."

He handed the photos to Clark. "Barge broke loose and slammed into the marina," Jimmy explained. "Doppelgänger tried to help, but everything he did made things worse."

Clark flipped through the pictures with growing apprehension. It was like a flip book of destruction.

"Until — there! See? That's my favorite shot," Jimmy said, pointing. "The doppelgänger's using superbreath to blow out the fire. And it worked!"

"Good," Clark muttered. He didn't know whether to be glad or sorry that the monster had yet another one of his superpowers.

"Of course, if the doppelgänger hadn't been there,

the fire probably wouldn't have started in the first place. Miss Lane said —"

"Olsen, where's Lois?" Perry growled. He practically snatched the stack of photos from Clark's hands and began flipping through them rapidly. "What — no shots of Superman?"

"Uh . . . Superman didn't show, Chief!" Jimmy looked around wildly, as if he hoped Lois would appear magically beside him. "Lois said she just had to do an interview. There were guys covering this thing for other media. Big surprise, huh? I guess she wanted an exclusive. With . . . somebody," he finished lamely.

"Well, in fifteen minutes, she'll have missed the final deadline," Perry growled. "Olsen, you were there. Talk to Kent. Kent, write up what we have!"

Perry stalked back into his office.

Clark and Jimmy looked at each other and shrugged. Knowing Lois, she'd probably dash in at the last minute. But orders were orders.

Jimmy riffled through the piles on Lois's desk. Finally, he pulled a folder with *Dop-Cad-SS* scrawled across the front.

"Lois was keeping this on the doppelgänger," Jimmy said, handing it to Clark. "It might have some background information."

Clark opened it.

The top paper had a single word scrawled across it in marker: *Cadmus?*

Interesting, Clark thought. *That would explain . . .*

Below were several pages of scrawled notes.

Clark glanced at them and saw they covered an interview with a Cadmus scientist named Welles about the alleged space signal.

Clark smiled. Lois's filing system was quirky to say the least. Anything remotely pertaining to Cadmus was stuffed in a single file. Still, she did seem to find things.

He was about to close the folder when the words "Krypton" and "distress signal" jumped off the page at him. He had begun to scan at superspeed when Jimmy interrupted him.

"Um. Now that I think about it, I wonder. You don't think maybe Miss Lane could be trying to interview the Superman doppelgänger, do you?"

11

Lois had flown with Superman numerous times and had always felt safe in his arms.

But flying with Bizarro was a nerve-wracking experience, full of drops, lurches, and sharp turns to avoid running into things. Lois breathed a sigh of relief when the mountains that enclosed Project Cadmus came into sight.

"Where we go now?" Bizarro asked.

"Metallo said you were supposed to kidnap me to lure Superman to him, right?" Lois asked. "Where were you supposed to take me?"

Bizarro hovered in the sky. "Me not sure. Metallo say come in hole, but me not see hole anymore. Me just see trees and rocks and dirt. And under that am wall."

"That's because this place is Superman-proof," Lois

explained. "It's lined with lead. So Superman can't see in."

"Or out," Bizarro said suddenly. "When me in lab, can't see out to sky. Me am . . . born in lab. Me think."

"That sounds right," Lois murmured. "Look, let's just fly around and see if we can find the place where the hole used to be." Lois thought for a minute. "Let's find the place where the meteor smashed through the mountain into Cadmus."

Bizarro frowned. "What am meteor?"

"A big rock that fell out of the sky. You probably weren't . . . born yet," Lois explained. "That's why you don't remember."

Bizarro flew low, practically skimming the treetops.

"There!" Lois pointed to an open space where toppled trees and raw rocks and dirt scarred the mountainside. "Look with your X-ray vision. Right there!"

Bizarro squinted at the rubble. Then he smiled.

"Me see hole," he said happily. "It just covered with a little dirt. All me have to do is dig."

Bizarro landed with a jolt. Carefully, he put Lois on the ground beside him.

103

He bent over and started to dig with his bare hands at superspeed, like a dog digging for a bone. Dirt flew out in an arc behind him.

⊶ ⊶ ⊶

Seismographs placed around the Project Cadmus complex picked up the disturbance as Bizarro began to tunnel, but Metallo silenced their warning signals with a thought.

Within the corridor, cameras swiveled to catch Bizarro's impending arrival, but Metallo stopped their feed to anyone but himself. Instead, he activated video loops of calm, empty spaces. Cadmus's human watchdogs would see only what Metallo wanted them to see.

At the same time, Metallo sent out orders to anyone who might have a reason to use that corridor. He wanted to keep all Cadmus employees away. Then he watched. And waited.

SMASH! Bizarro broke through the newly installed cement ceiling. He dropped through the hole and into the hall.

Where was the Lane woman? For a moment, Metallo was disappointed.

Then Lois Lane fell through the hole and into Bizarro's arms.

Lois looked around at the corridor. Several days ago, the corridor had been blocked by rubble. People had died here.

Now the rubble was gone, and the ceiling was repaired. The hallway stretched ahead, a blank, brightly lit expanse.

Lois frowned. "Where is everybody?"

Bizarro shrugged. "Metallo keep people away. Metallo say he control Cadmus now. Soon control all of Metropolis."

"How far is it?" Lois asked.

"Down hall, turn left, first room," Bizarro said. "Metallo make me memorize way."

As Lois and Bizarro walked down the deserted corridor, Lois noticed that the cameras mounted on the wall swiveled to follow their every movement.

Clark couldn't tell who was more anxious to get away from the Daily Planet bullpen — he or Jimmy.

They finished writing up the Boat Basin article in record time. Jimmy seemed so distracted that Clark took a chance and typed faster than was humanly possible.

In five minutes flat, Clark hit the command that sent the article to Perry's desk computer. "Done!" he said.

"Great! Well, uh, bye, Mr. Kent," Jimmy said as he backed toward his desk. "Gotta go! See you!"

Jimmy grabbed his camera and bolted out through the bullpen doors.

Clark watched with X-ray vision until Jimmy was in the elevator, heading down. Then he rushed for the stairs.

Less than a minute later, Superman burst out the access door onto the roof.

As he leaped into the air, the loud roar of an engine caught his attention. Down below, Jimmy Olsen was riding his motorcycle out of the Daily Planet building parking garage and into traffic. He watched as Jimmy roared off, heading for the Queensland Bridge.

As Superman sped toward the mountains, he hoped Jimmy would reach Project Cadmus in time to get the pictures he wanted.

Because if Lois was a captive inside Cadmus, the fight to end all fights was about to begin.

Metallo watched as Bizarro led the Lane woman down the empty corridor. They seemed to be cooperating, Metallo noted. And Lane appeared to be in charge.

A classic scenario of Beauty taming the Beast, Metallo thought with contempt. *The idiot construct has shifted his allegiance to Lois Lane.*

Metallo shrugged. After the fiasco in Suicide Slum and the Boat Basin, it was apparent that the Bizarro Mark 3 could never fulfill its primary function anyway.

He would have to destroy it.

Bizarro stepped into the laboratory and faced the being who had created him. Lois hesitated in the open doorway behind him.

"Miss Lane," Metallo said in a mechanized voice. "Come in. I've been expecting you."

She stepped into the room, staring in horror and amazement at the gleaming robot.

I knew something was going on at Cadmus, she thought. *But this is weirder than I imagined.*

Bizarro glanced back at her. "Lois, this am Metallo."

The robot gazed at Lois from lidless silver eyes set in a gleaming metal skull. Chrome-sheathed muscles covered its man-shaped skeleton. But the robot didn't move like a man. Its gestures were too swift and fluid, more reptilian than human.

Lois folded her arms. Metallo terrified her, but she wouldn't let it see her fear.

"Superman isn't coming, Metallo. He doesn't have a clue I'm here. So you might as well forget about using me as bait," she said.

Metallo turned his head and stared directly at the construct. "I see Bizarro has been telling you my little secrets." For an instant, the pupil of his eyes seemed to glow an eerie green.

Lois frowned. "Bizarro? Is that what you call him?"

She glanced at the large, pale creature standing beside her. Bizarro had begun to slump. His skin was looking sweaty and had a greenish tint. *What's wrong with him?* she wondered.

Metallo shrugged. "It's what the project that created him is called. And what that creature is. To be exact, it is a Bizarro Mark 3."

Metallo spread his arms, inviting her to study him.

"Looks can be deceiving, Miss Lane. I appear to be a robot. But in reality, I am a man with a prosthetic body.

"This —" He gestured with a silver hand toward Bizarro, "appears to be a man . . . of sorts. But it is actually a kind of robot, made up of billions of nanoparticles — molecule-sized machines that mimic human or, in this case, Kryptonian, function.

"Bizarro Mark 3 is my finest creation . . . so far."

This time, Lois was sure she saw Metallo's eyes spark green.

Bizarro bent over and clutched at his stomach. "Me

know . . . already . . . me am not real Superman. Now you say . . . me am not real . . . anything." He fell to his knees. "Why you do this? Why you . . . make me?"

"If I told you, I'd have to kill you! Oh. That's right. I *am* killing you!" A sound like the squeaking of a rusted hinge came from Metallo's speakers. Lois guessed it was supposed to be a laugh.

Bizarro toppled onto the floor. He rolled onto his side and lay still.

Lois knelt beside him. "Why?"

Metallo shrugged. "Bizarro was created to take Superman's place once that alien *monster* . . . that extra-terrestrial *fiend* was destroyed. He is clearly inadequate for that task!"

Alien monster . . . extraterrestrial fiend. Lois frowned. That sounded familiar. Someone had just said —

Her mind flashed through a series of images. The damaged Cadmus corridor beginning to collapse. Superman trying to hold the ceiling up. The gray-haired doctor choosing to die rather than accept Superman's help.

Lois stared in horror at the silver robot. Was it possible? Was that *really* an artificial body? And if it was . . .

"Then you didn't die after all, Dr. Vale?"

"Unexpectedly perceptive, Miss Lane! Maybe you're as good as they say you are," Metallo said.

"I eavesdropped on your interview with that radio astronomer Welles," he continued. "I know there are other Kryptonians alive. That they are sending signals to Earth. And that Superman will return to Krypton and lead his alien allies in an invasion —"

"What?" Lois gaped at Metallo. "That isn't true. It's a mistake . . . or a hoax. Welles *claims* he's heard this distress signal, but I couldn't find a similar report from any other reputable scientist."

"You would say or do anything to protect your alien lover, wouldn't you, Miss Lane? Even betray your own kind," Metallo said. "Well, soon you'll have the chance to die with him."

Lois sneered. "What makes you think you can kill Superman?"

Metallo glanced pointedly at the fallen Bizarro. "I really don't think that will be a problem!"

12

As Superman hovered above Project Cadmus, he listened with superhearing attuned to Lois's voice. And, knowing X-ray vision was useless here, he searched the area with heat-seeking thermal vision for any clue to her whereabouts.

He spotted a column of heat rising from the far side of the mountain, shining like a beacon in the cool night air.

He was off like a shot.

⊶ ⊶ ⊶

Through his interface with the Cadmus external cameras, Metallo watched as Superman hovered warily over Bizarro's tunnel.

Don't you realize it's too late for caution? Metallo

thought contemptuously. *It's time to take this to the next level.*

His silver hand shot out, quick as a snake, and grabbed Lois's dark shoulder-length hair.

"Ow!" she screamed. "Let me go!"

He dragged her to the door and into the corridor beyond.

"Superman!" Lois shouted. "Keep away! It's a trap."

Metallo looked at her with gleaming eyes. "Thank you for calling him, Miss Lane," he said. "Here he comes now!"

Metallo was filled with excitement. Before using the ultimate weapon to destroy his enemy, he planned to test his other powers — his ability to control Cadmus's computerized defenses, and his own strength and invulnerability — against this enemy of Earth.

He could barely wait.

Superman was in the tunnel like a shot.

KLANG! KLANG! Bars shot down from the ceiling, before and behind him, enclosing him.

At the end of the hall stood Lois.

Beside her was a gleaming robot, with one of its clawlike hands tangled in her dark hair.

And beyond them, Superman saw the doppelgänger lying on the floor of a lab in a near-lifeless heap.

Who's the robot? Superman wondered. *What the heck is going on here?*

"It's Vale," Lois shouted. "The doctor who wouldn't leave the tunnel. He's had his brain transferred into that . . . thing!"

"Miss Lane!" The robot jerked her head back sharply. "If you must introduce me, call me by my proper name. Call me Metallo!"

"This is stupid, Metallo!" Superman shouted. "You know steel bars won't cage me."

He grabbed the bars, jerked them apart with a single motion, and stepped through them, setting off blaring alarms.

"So much for secrecy!" Superman said.

"But I don't want your trespass to be secret," Metallo said. "The surveillance tapes will verify that you broke into Cadmus. And that you took out our defenses."

Laser weapons popped down from the ceiling. They swiveled and locked on Superman.

PZAAAPT! PZAPT! ZAPPPT! Narrow beams of light shot from their barrels . . . and bounced off of Superman's chest.

"It's called invulnerability!" Superman said grimly. He walked through the laser barrage, casually blasting the lasers apart with heat vision.

Then he focused his heat vision on Metallo's chest. The metal there began to glow white hot but it didn't melt.

"Better and better," the robot croaked as Superman stalked toward him. "The government will see this attack, like your erratic behavior in Suicide Slum and the Boat Basin, as proof of your madness."

"You know that was Bizarro!" Lois shouted to be heard over the blaring alarms.

"But Miss Lane, I read all about it in the *Times*!" Metallo taunted. Abruptly, he pushed Lois in front of him.

Heart in his throat, Superman shut off his heat vision before Lois was burned.

"I think that's an adequate test of the alloy from which my body is built!" Metallo said, and laughed his rusty-hinge laugh. "Like it? It's my own invention."

The robot's had the upper hand for too long, Lois thought. It was time to shake his control.

"In case you hadn't noticed, Superman, Metallo's the one who's mad. He hates you. But he's an idiot. He built Bizarro — the doppelgänger — actually thinking it could take your place. He says you're an alien monster. But he's —"

"Enough!" Metallo yanked Lois onto her toes. He looked right at Superman. "I am what I chose to be. It takes a monster to kill a monster."

And his eyes flashed an eerie green.

A sudden wave of weakness nearly knocked Superman off his feet. For an instant, darkness shrouded his vision. With an effort of will, he forced himself back to consciousness.

What was happening to him?

Jimmy Olsen's motorcyle was pushing eighty as it sped up the mountain road. With the rumble of the motor and the wind roaring past his helmet, Jimmy almost missed the shriek of the alarm.

He pulled his bike to the side of the road and yanked off his helmet to listen. The noise was coming from somewhere up the mountain.

From Cadmus? he wondered. *What else could it be?*

He squinted up the wooded slope. He thought he saw a wash of light on the trees about a hundred yards above him.

He grabbed his camera from the saddlebags on the back of the bike.

Then, wishing he'd thought to bring a flashlight, he began to climb through the brush, past trees, and over rocks toward the source of the noise.

Above the blaring alarm, Metallo could hear shouts and the clatter of feet as Cadmus scientists and guards converged on the corridor.

At his mental command, iron bars at either end of the corridor slammed down from the ceiling, blocking their access.

Cadmus workers pressed against the bars, shouting questions.

"What's happening?"

"What's Superman doing here?"

"Where'd that robot come from?"

"It's got Lois Lane!"

Several guards raised their weapons, looking confused. "Who do we shoot? Superman or the robot?" one of them asked.

"My brother was in this corridor and Superman saved him," another muttered. "I say we take down the robot."

"Hold your fire!" Metallo shouted. "Superman has become dangerously unstable. He and his girlfriend here just broke into Cadmus! He's dangerous!"

"And what are you?" a guard asked suspiciously, weapon pointed at Metallo.

"I am a top-secret Cadmus artifact designed to deal with this situation," Metallo said smoothly. "If you'll check your orders, you'll see that I have been given full authorization to act."

Metallo concentrated . . . and the orders appeared on the leader's handheld Cadmus Digital Assistant screen.

The leader nodded warily. "It's right," he said. "Stand down."

The guards lowered their weapons.

"Now that we have witnesses, our final battle will begin," Metallo said softly, for Superman's ears alone. "They'll see Cadmus's champion fight the mad alien and destroy him. End of story."

"He's lying!" Lois shouted to the watching crowd. "He's —"

Metallo flung Lois hard against the wall.

"No!" Superman staggered forward.

Metallo looked at Superman. Again his eyes flashed green.

Superman stumbled. He felt a pain in his gut. He blinked, trying to shake off his mind-numbing confusion. Something was very wrong.

Then, suddenly, he understood.

"Kryptonite!" he whispered.

"Kryptonite radiation, actually," Metallo said. "Focused as rays through my eyes. Now that we understand each other, alien, let the games begin!"

13

Metallo swung at Superman with a gleaming fist.

Superman ducked and the blow grazed his shoulder. A quick glance at Lois, sprawled against the wall, showed him she was still breathing.

He hit Metallo with an uppercut, and Metallo staggered back. But only a few feet.

Superman's knuckles throbbed from the contact. As the kryptonite poisoned his body, his superpowers were fading.

He hit Metallo again with all his remaining strength. Metallo slammed into the wall but remained upright. His eyes began to flash a deadly green.

Not good! Superman thought. He dove to the left, but he wasn't fast enough. With the remains of his full-spectrum vision, he saw the poisonous radioactivity rake his right ankle.

Fire seared up his leg, and he toppled to the floor.

Losing power. Got to take him out now! Superman thought. *Need to keep behind him, away from his eyes.*

With a last, desperate lunge, he swept his left leg out and knocked Metallo off his feet.

With a clang, Metallo crashed to the floor next to Lois.

The robot grabbed her hair. "One hard twist and her neck will snap. Probably she'll die. If not, she could end up like me! The Bride of Metallo . . . what do you think?"

"No . . . ," she groaned. She opened her eyes and tried to pull away.

"No!" Superman crawled toward them. "Let her go!"

"Closer," Metallo said. "Closer. Close enough!"

At Metallo's mental command, doors in his chest cavity swung wide, exposing the glowing green rock that powered his body.

Eerie green radiation pulsed from his chest and bathed the room in poison.

Ripped by agony, Superman fell face forward on the floor.

Metallo rose, towering over Superman, and jerked a groggy Lois up beside him.

He kicked Superman over onto his back, then reached into his own chest cavity and pulled out the glowing crystal. On its surface was the raised letter *M*.

"Do you see this, Superman?" he asked. "I thought it would be an appropriate way to mark my victories."

Lois was beginning to recover. She pushed Metallo, kicked and shoved at his arm, but he was too strong.

Slowly, savoring his moment of triumph, Metallo lowered the kryptonite toward Superman's forehead.

Then, without warning, Metallo lurched sideways and slammed onto the concrete floor, dragging Lois crashing down with him. Instinctively, Metallo opened his hands to break his fall.

The kryptonite crystal skidded across the floor.

And Lois was free.

"Metallo bad!" Bizarro's voice boomed. "You not hurt Lois! You not hurt Superman!"

Lois looked over and saw that Bizarro had tackled Metallo to the ground.

Bizarro was back in the lab, Lois realized. *Away from the poisonous kryptonite. He must have recovered, at least partially.*

Now, exposed anew, Bizarro's skin was turning gray. His grip on Metallo slackened.

Metallo kicked out at Bizarro, shoving him away. "You useless pile of nanoparticles! Did you really think I would build a new Superman without including Superman's great weakness? What else would protect the world from *you*?"

"Maybe me am useless, but am tough," Bizarro said. "Me not good to save people. But me save Superman."

Bizarro lurched to his feet and threw himself on top of the kryptonite.

His dense body blocked the radiation from the rest of the room. "Go . . . Superman." Bizarro gasped out. "Save Lois. Stop Metallo. Bad . . ."

Superman felt a pulse of energy as his powers began to return. He pushed himself to his knees.

Checking with X-ray vision, he saw the kryptonite had already burned a hole in Bizarro's chest. The creature's artificial heart and lungs were damaged beyond repair. He had given his life to save Superman and Lois. And to stop Metallo.

Superman would see that his sacrifice was not in vain.

Metallo lunged for Bizarro, planning to kick him over and retrieve the kryptonite, but Superman was faster.

He tackled Metallo around the waist and leaped up through the hole in the ceiling, away from the kryptonite and into the night air.

Jimmy, puffing a bit from his steep climb, peered up over a rock ledge into a clearing strewn with rocks and fallen trees. Farther back was a hole in the ground with light shining out of it.

"Holy cow!" Jimmy muttered as Superman and a gleaming skull-faced robot shot out of the hole. Superman had the robot by the waist.

Supes must have tackled him, Jimmy thought.

Then the robot kicked out, breaking Superman's hold. Superman and robot tumbled to the ground.

"Not much light," Jimmy muttered. "Luckily my

film's fast. Gonna have to make the aperture wide open. I don't think Superman would appreciate a flash!"

Jimmy took shot after shot as Superman hit the robot with an uppercut to the jaw. The robot staggered back a few steps, then kicked out, delivering a glancing blow to Superman's ribs.

Either Superman's giving that robot a break or the robot's incredibly strong, Jimmy thought. *Whatever is going on, though, the pictures are going to be stellar.*

"Man of Steel versus Man of Steel!" Jimmy muttered. He could practically see the headline. And, beneath it, taking up the top half of page one — his own iconic shot of Superman.

At first Superman struggled to hold his own against Metallo. He had barely been able to carry the heavy robot outside. But the longer he was away from the kryptonite, the more his powers returned.

He began to block Metallo's blows. And to hit the robot harder. It wasn't a boxing match so much as a down and dirty street fight.

"You think you're Metropolis's hero, but the truth is you're alien scum . . . an invading monster . . . and the government of this great country wants you gone," Metallo snarled.

He head-butted Superman in the gut, knocking him to the ground.

Superman grabbed Metallo and pushed the robot's head back . . . farther . . . farther . . .

"Who do you think financed this operation?" Metallo continued. "Do you think Project Cadmus tried to destroy you for fun? We were paid . . . and paid well!"

"You're lying!" Superman shouted. With a furious shove, he ripped the robot's head from its neck.

No longer under Metallo's control, the body collapsed on top of Superman like a puppet whose strings had been cut.

But the head, rolling onto the rubble-strewn ground, kept on talking. "The fact that you beat me, their greatest weapon against you, will only increase their certainty that you're a potential threat and must be destroyed!"

127

The fight was over.

Jimmy thought about sticking around. But Cadmus employed big goons with big guns whose jobs were to keep guys like him from taking pictures of their operations.

He decided to escape while his camera was still intact.

He grinned as he slipped quietly down the hill toward his motorcycle. He was pretty sure Superman and Miss Lane could handle it from here.

❈   ❈   ❈

Superman looked down, searching the corridor below for Metallo's chunk of kryptonite.

He saw Lois kneeling beside the dying Bizarro. And the Cadmus personnel still held at bay behind the barred gates.

Finally, he spotted the kryptonite behind the closed door of the lab where Lois must have tossed it. Only then did he drop through the hole in the ceiling, back into Cadmus.

He was holding Metallo's skull-like head, which was finally, blessedly quiet.

He walked over and knelt beside Lois and Bizarro — the being he had thought of as a monster. He alone could fully understand the agony Bizarro was feeling . . . and appreciate the true extent of his sacrifice.

Perhaps it was the effect of the kryptonite radiation on the nanoparticles that made up his body. But as they watched, Bizarro began to slowly dissolve. First fingers, then hands, then arms. Death, moving inexorably onward.

"Do not cry, Lois!" he croaked. "Bizarro am not real human person!"

"What they call you doesn't matter," Lois said. "What matters is what's in your heart. What matters is that you're a true hero. And worthy . . ." Lois's voice clogged with tears.

". . . worthy of sharing the name of Superman!" Superman finished.

Bizarro smiled, a gentle childlike smile . . . that faded finally into dust.

14

Under protest from Cadmus officials, Superman had turned Metallo's head over to the Metropolis's maximum security internment center on Strykers Island.

He had few illusions. He knew that if the United States government wanted Metallo's head, they would get it. He had the horrible feeling that he had not seen the last of that mad robot.

As he flew over the West River between New Troy and Queensland Park carrying Lois in his arms, his scowl deepened.

Vale didn't even know me, he thought. *And yet he hated me so much that he would destroy himself in order to destroy me.*

"I can't believe it! Our government . . . our own

government used taxpayers' money to commission that madman to duplicate and destroy me!" he said. "Is that the way they see me? As some kind of dangerous alien fiend?"

Lois frowned. "It can't be the whole government. Maybe a few crazies. I thought I saw Senator Buckram of Texas in the Cadmus corridors during the meteor shower. He's fanatic enough. And he's a bigwig in military appropriations. There's all sorts of secret stuff hidden in that budget. I wonder —"

Lois was lost in thought as they flew back to the Daily Planet building. Superman knew she was planning her article. And considering her next big exposé.

"Good job, Olsen!" Perry White said as he handed Jimmy the morning edition of the *Daily Planet*.

The headline read MAN OF STEEL VS. MAN OF STEEL, just as Jimmy had imagined. His photograph showed Superman grappling with the robot Metallo. And beneath it was Jimmy's byline.

It was a daydream come true.

"Now I want you to get down to City Hall," Perry said. "The mayor's gonna make a statement about this Cadmus mess."

"Yeah. Okay, Chief," Jimmy said. He grabbed his camera.

"Where's Olsen going?" Jack Green complained. "I need somebody to run this obit photo down to layout."

"Do it yourself," Perry told him. "Olsen's just been promoted to staff photographer."

Lois sat at her desk, frowning at her notes about the radio signal from Krypton.

She was worried about Superman. He had seemed so . . . unsettled recently. The Cadmus thing had really gotten to him.

She couldn't find anything that suggested Dr. Welles was qualified to make such an assertion. Nor could she find another radio astronomer who would corroborate the story as a primary source. All reports led directly back to Dr. Welles.

And all his Kryptonian-signal nonsense had done was drive a madman to even greater heights of madness.

"I can't believe the *National Scientific* will actually publish this junk," Lois muttered.

She tossed the folder on her desk.

If the story gets published, I'll show Superman my data, she thought. *Otherwise, I'll just forget it. Right now, I've got much more important fish to fry.*

The thought that other Kryptonians might still be alive was eating at him. That they may have sent out a distress signal. That they might need his help.

I could go there, he thought for the hundredth time. *I should go there. Here on Earth, I'm hated . . . or loved because I'm different. It sets me apart. If there are others like me . . .*

If Lois and I are to have any hope of a life together, I'll have to tell her the truth.

And before I can do that, I need to go to Krypton and find out what that truth really is.

If Superman was going to Krypton, then Clark Kent would have to disappear as well.

"I've . . . come into an inheritance," Clark told Perry White. "I've decided to use it to take a trip. Around the world."

Perry humphed, not at all pleased that one of his top reporters was quitting on him.

"I can't promise your job will be waiting for you when you get back," Perry growled.

"I understand," Clark said.

❦ ❦ ❦

Lois was on the telephone when Clark stopped in front of her desk. She held up a finger.

"I want to ask you about Senator Buckram, of the Senate Select Committee on Military Appropriations . . . Lois Lane of the *Daily Planet*. About the Cadmus . . . Yes, I'll hold. . . ."

She put a hand over the phone and looked up at Clark inquiringly.

"Lois, I'm leaving the *Planet* to travel. Around . . ." He made a circling motion with his finger.

"The world? What, right now?" Lois looked at him like he'd lost his mind.

He shrugged. "It's spur of the moment. Kind of a once-in-a-lifetime deal."

"Well, hey, congratulations! We'll miss you! You told Jimmy? I bet he's heartbroken!"

"Jimmy's too busy to be —"

She held up her finger, cutting him off as someone came back on the line. "Yes. Senator Buckram. No. Project Cadmus . . ."

Clark pointed toward the bullpen doors, miming that he had to leave now.

Lois stood and gave him a quick hug and peck on the cheek. She never took the phone away from her ear.

As Clark walked out through the bullpen doors, Perry was dragging a tall, dark-haired man from out of the adjoining office.

"Richard!" Perry said, "I want you to meet Lois Lane. . . ."

They met one final time on the Daily Planet roof.

Lois talked on and on about Senator Buckram and Cadmus-gate. Two other senators had been implicated. . . .

Superman sighed. Lois knew the Cadmus fiasco had upset him and probably thought her unflagging investigation would make him feel better.

But, for some reason, it no longer interested him.

It's better this way, he told himself. How could he stay on Earth to please her? How could he not?

Superman straightened. "I have to go," he said.

Why am I acting like this is the end of life as we know it? Superman wondered. *I shouldn't be away for more than a few months. And when I get back, I'll know what to say to her.*

Superman leaned down and kissed her. "Take care," he said.

"I always do. Well, sort of." Lois grinned and stepped back. "You take care, too!"

"Yeah!" Superman gazed down at her, memorizing the curve of her smile, and the curl of her hair, and the texture of her skin. "Just," he said hesitantly, "do me a favor and be a little more careful from now on. Okay?"

There was something in his eyes Lois didn't remember ever seeing before, almost a sadness. "Okay." She wondered for a moment what it was they were saying to each other.

Then he stepped back, leaped into the sky, and flew north toward his Fortress of Solitude.

The crystalline rocket ship he would take into space grew in a matter of hours, attached to an antechamber in his Fortress. The programming was within the Master Crystal. He had only to tell the crystal what he needed.

Mom promised to get my friends around the world to send postcards to Lois and Jimmy for me . . . until I get back, he thought absently as he waited. *That should preserve my Clark Kent identity until —*

"Krypton was destroyed, Kal-El!" his father's voice said behind him. "Only shards of the planet are left and those shards will have been irradiated by the destroyed red sun. No one could have survived that disaster! No one is left."

"You aren't truly my father," Superman said. "You're an image of him, programmed before you sent me away in the rocket. You can't know what happened."

You're an illusion, he thought. *Like so much of my life has been an illusion. I need to know what's real. What's true. I need to see for myself.*

But Krypton had been irradiated. That much was fact. He knew, from personal experience, what kryptonite could do to him.

So he strode from the Fortress of Solitude and leaped into the air. He flew straight up into the stratosphere, where the yellow sun bathed his body in warmth and power.

⊷ ⊷ ⊷

When he returned to the Fortress, the crystal ship was waiting for him — beautiful, alien, pulsing with light.

He felt a jolt of anticipation. Or was it dread?

He took off his blue-and-red Superman suit, and put on a gray cold-sleep bodysuit. To preserve the power he had absorbed, he would travel to his home world in suspended animation.

138

"It's time," he said.

A door in the side of the ship slid open and he stepped inside.

"Home," he ordered. "To Krypton!"

Silently the door slid shut behind him.

He lay on the cold-sleep couch and watched the crystal cover close above him.

He felt a slight rocking as the ship climbed into space.

Then he closed his eyes. And slept.

Epilogue

The winter wind plastered Lois's coat to her back and whipped her hair into streamers as she stood on the roof of the Daily Planet building, staring into the night sky. The famous globe was spotlit and the city lights were bright around her. Only a few stars were visible.

Was *he* out there somewhere among them?

"Where are you?" she whispered. "Why did you go? Were you really saying good-bye?

She took a drag on her cigarette and blew smoke into the wind. She had so much to tell him. There was so much she wanted him to know.

"You shouldn't smoke," a voice said. "It's not good for you."

Lois looked up — for one shining moment, she'd thought it was his voice.

Then she saw it was Richard White. He left the shelter of the access door and walked over to lean against the rampart beside her.

She shrugged ruefully. "I gave up smoking a while back. But recently . . . I started up again. The stress, I guess."

Lois reached in her pocket and clutched the meteorite — the one Superman had given her — like a talisman. She looked skyward as if she could read the answer in the stars.

She looks too thin, Richard thought. *She isn't eating. She isn't taking care of herself. Perry's worried about her. I'm . . . worried.*

"Have you had dinner?" he asked abruptly.

"Dinner?"

"Yeah. You know, you go to a restaurant and sit at a table and a waiter brings you whatever delicious thing you want to eat." He grinned devilishly.

She couldn't stop herself from grinning back. "I've heard of that," she said.

"You've been kicking senatorial butt on that Cadmus exposé for weeks now," he coaxed. "Why don't you forget it for the night and let me buy you dinner?"

Lois glanced at the sky. Then she looked at Richard White, really looked at him for the first time.

"Yeah," she said. "Thanks. Dinner would be nice."